CHINCHILLA UP THE CHIMNEY

The bathroom door suddenly opened. 'Here's some lunch,' Mrs Hope said cheerfully, appearing with a tray of sandwiches and crisps.

Mandy gasped in dismay. The chinchilla froze for a second and then, dropping the raisin, streaked towards the door, its ears flat back, its tail flying out behind it.

'Oh!' cried Mrs Hope, almost dropping the tray as the chinchilla flew past her.

'Quick!' Mandy cried, leaping to her feet. 'We can't let it get away!'

The chinchilla dashed along the corridor and down the stairs with Mandy and James in close pursuit. They reached the sitting-room door just in time to see it racing towards the large stone fireplace.

'Oh no!' Mandy gasped, realising where it was heading.

With one agile bound, the chinchilla leaped up the chimney. Mandy and James looked at each other.

What were they going to do *now*?

Animal Ark series

LUCY DANIELS

Chinchilla
—up the—
Chimney

Illustrations by Ann Baum

*Hodder
Children's
Books*

a division of Hodder Headline plc

To Katherine

Special thanks to Linda Chapman
Thanks also to C. J. Hall, B.Vet.Med., M.R.C.V.S., for reviewing
the veterinary information contained in this book.

Animal Ark is a trademark of Working Partners Limited
Text copyright © 1999 Working Partners Limited
Created by Working Partners Limited, London W6 0QT
Original series created by Ben M. Baglio
Illustrations copyright © 1999 Ann Baum

First published in Great Britain in 1999
by Hodder Children's Books

A Catalogue record for this book is available from the British Library

ISBN 0 340 73603 8

Typeset by Avon Dataset Ltd, Bidford-on-Avon, Warks

Printed and bound in Great Britain by
Clays Ltd, St Ives plc

Hodder Children's Books
a division of Hodder Headline plc
338 Euston Road
London NW1 3BH

One

Mandy watched as a tiny pink nose emerged from a bundle of bedding. Long whiskers twitched inquisitively for a moment and then out popped a pointed white head. The mouse scampered across the cage and over to the food bowl. Mandy smiled and breathed in the heavy smell of fish food and birdseed that hung in the stuffy air. She loved visiting the pet shop. A second white mouse came out from the nest to join the first.

'Shall we go?' A voice interrupted her thoughts.

Mandy looked round. James Hunter, her best friend, was coming over from the counter with the packet of dog chews he had just bought.

'Look, James. Aren't they lovely?' Mandy pointed to the mice.

James grinned as he stuffed the packet of chews into his school bag. They were for his Labrador, Blackie. 'You think all animals are lovely!'

'So do you!' Mandy retorted.

James shifted his bag on to his shoulder and pushed his glasses back up his nose. He *was* just as keen on animals as Mandy. 'Come on!' he said. 'Let's get home.'

Mandy followed him reluctantly to the door. She could have stayed in the pet shop for hours. She had already decided that when she left school she wanted to be a vet, like her parents, but she thought working in a pet shop would be one of the next best things.

'Bye!' called Geoff, the pet shop owner. 'Have a good half-term!'

'Thanks!' Mandy called back. She liked Geoff. He never minded how often she came in to look at the animals and when he wasn't busy with customers he was always keen to chat.

'I hope the weather stays like this,' James said, as he opened the door and they stepped into the bright May sunshine. 'Just think, no more school for a whole week. We can play tennis and go swimming.'

'And eat loads of ice cream,' said Mandy longingly. She was feeling hot in her school trousers and not looking forward to the two-mile bike ride home to Welford, the village where they lived. Still, at least they were on half-term now!

Collecting their bikes from the bike rack, they wheeled them on to the road. They were just setting off when Mandy noticed Jean Knox, the receptionist at Animal Ark, her mum and dad's veterinary surgery, waiting by the bus stop. 'There's Jean!' she said in surprise to James. 'What's she doing at the bus stop? Where's her car?'

They cycled over. 'Jean!' Mandy called.

Jean looked round, the confused look clearing from her face as she recognised Mandy and James. 'Hello, dears,' she said.

'Where's your car?' Mandy asked, looking at

the sea of shopping bags that surrounded Jean's feet.

'In the garage, having its MOT done,' Jean explained. She patted her grey hair. 'It's so silly of me. I forgot it was due today and as I'm going on holiday next week I had to come in by bus to get everything.' She shook her head. 'I don't know why I didn't remember.'

Mandy exchanged looks with James. Jean was always forgetting things. It didn't surprise her at all that Jean had forgotten to have her car's MOT test done in time.

'Here's the bus,' James pointed out to Jean as a blue-and-yellow vehicle came round the corner and down the road towards them. Jean started to gather up her bags.

Suddenly the door of one of the nearby houses flew open and a black cat came racing out, followed by an old man. 'Go on! Get out of here!' he shouted, shaking his fist angrily.

'No!' gasped Mandy in horror as the cat ran straight across the pavement and into the road. It escaped the wheels of the bus by mere centimetres, streaking away to the safety of the opposite pavement.

Mandy's breath left her in one trembling rush. Thank goodness! She looked round and saw the old man going back into his house. Dropping her bike, she ran over to him. 'What did you do that for?' she cried. 'That cat could have been run over!'

'What?' The old man swung round. His face was small and wizened like an old apple but his blue eyes were sharp.

'That cat almost got hit!' Mandy exclaimed. She couldn't believe the old man's apparent lack of concern. James, who had run after her, put a restraining hand on her arm but she took no notice.

'Mind your own business!' The old man stomped back into the house and slammed the door.

Mandy stared after him. 'Well!' she exclaimed, swinging round and looking at James indignantly. 'What's the matter with *him*?'

James shrugged. 'It's not worth getting upset about,' he said, in his usual practical way. 'The cat's not hurt, and he obviously just doesn't like animals.' He looked to where she had dropped her bike on the pavement. 'I hope your bike's OK.' He hurried over.

Mandy followed him more slowly. She was still recovering from the shock of the unpleasant incident. She glanced over her shoulder. What an unpleasant man!

The next instant, all thoughts of the old man disappeared from her mind. There was something small shooting down the pavement towards her. It was a very strange-looking animal – light brown, about the size of a small rabbit, with a long, bushy tail. Before Mandy knew what had happened, it had dashed past her and was racing straight towards the queue of people who were stepping on to the bus. Its large, round ears were flat against its head in panic. *What is it?* Mandy wondered. *It's not a rabbit or a rat or a squirrel.* The next instant, the animal reached the bus and disappeared among Jean's carrier bags.

Totally oblivious to what had just happened, Jean picked up her carrier bags and got on to the bus. The doors hissed shut behind her.

'James!' Mandy gasped.

James looked up, his eyes widening in surprise as he saw the expression on Mandy's face. 'What?' he demanded.

But Mandy knew she didn't have the time to explain. She started running towards the bus. 'Jean!' she shouted; but it was too late. As she started running, the bus pulled out into the road. Mandy's eyes scanned the pavement but there was no sign of the strange animal. It must be on the bus!

'Wait!' Mandy cried, speeding up. The bus was stuck behind a slow-moving car – maybe she could catch it! 'Jean!' she shouted desperately as she saw Jean sit down on the back seat and put her bags down beside her.

Jean looked round. Seeing Mandy running behind the bus she waved cheerfully then settled back down in her seat.

A sandy-coloured head suddenly popped up out of one of the bags on the back seat. Two black eyes, wide and frightened, looked at Mandy and then with a nervous jump the animal dived back into the safety of the bag, leaving Mandy with just a quick glimpse of a squirrel-like tail.

Mandy stopped, panting for breath as the bus overtook the car and disappeared down the road.

'Mandy!' James came hurrying up with their two bikes. His astonished eyes scanned her face. 'What's up with you?'

Mandy's words came out in a gabble. 'James! There's an animal in one of Jean's carrier bags!'

James looked at her as if he thought she'd gone mad. 'What sort of an animal?' he asked.

Mandy hesitated for a moment. Had it been what she thought? 'I *think* it was a chinchilla,' she stammered.

'A chinchilla!' James echoed.

Mandy nodded. She had only seen one once before at Animal Ark, but she was sure she recognised the big, round ears and the fluffy body. She grabbed her bike from him. 'It must have jumped into one of Jean's bags just as she was getting on to the bus. We've got to catch up with her.'

'But . . .'

'Come on!' Mandy saw the bus reach a bend in the road ahead. If it *was* a chinchilla then it certainly wouldn't survive if it escaped into the wild! She jumped on to her bike. 'If we're quick we might manage it.'

She started pedalling frantically down the

road. Not bothering to argue any more, James jumped on his bike and followed her.

By the time they reached the corner, the bus was chugging up the steep hill that led out of Walton. Gritting her teeth, Mandy stood up on her pedals and forced her legs to go as fast as they could. She ignored the banging of her heart and the sweat that was streaming down her hot face. Glancing over her shoulder she saw James just behind. His face was pink and

his glasses were halfway down his nose but his mouth was set in a determined line. Good old James! Mandy pushed on up the last few metres of the hill.

Reaching the top, her heart leaped. The bus was only halfway down the other side. Gasping for breath she let her bike freewheel as fast as it could.

The rushing air whipped the sweat from her face as she flew down the road. The red brake lights of the bus flashed on as the driver braked to slow the descent. Mandy got closer and closer. 'Stop!' she tried to shout, but her breath was coming in gasps and she could hardly get the words out. No one on the bus looked round.

As the bus reached the bottom of the hill, the driver suddenly accelerated again. In despair, Mandy watched as it pulled away from her. By the time she reached the top of the next hill the bus was already halfway up the following one.

She stopped for a moment and James caught up with her. 'We've lost it!' she panted in dismay. 'We'll *never* catch it now.'

'If we keep it in sight, we can stop Jean when

she gets off in Welford,' said James, fixing his glasses more firmly on to his nose. 'Come on!'

They set off again. Cycling hard, they managed to keep the bus in view, gaining on it slightly as they flew downhill and losing it again on the slow climbs upwards.

'Only this one to go!' gasped Mandy as they reached the bottom of the last hill before Welford. The bus reached the crest of the hill and disappeared from view.

Mandy cycled up the agonising last few metres. Hope started to flow through her. If they could catch Jean at the bus stop they could rescue the chinchilla from her bag and then hopefully find its owner. 'Almost there!' she called over her shoulder to James.

She reached the top of the hill and screeched to an abrupt stop.

A flock of sheep filled the road. A farmer was standing by an open field gate herding them out with the help of two Border collies. 'Afternoon!' he called cheerfully. 'Sorry to hold you up!'

Mandy stared in dismay as the blue-and-yellow bus disappeared into the village below.

Two

It seemed to take for ever for the farmer to get all the sheep out of one field and into another a little further down the road. Calling a hasty goodbye, Mandy and James sped off anxiously down the hill – but when they reached the bus stop at the Fox and Goose crossroads there was no sign of Jean or the bus.

'What do we do now?' James said, looking round.

Mandy saw Mr Hardy, the landlord of the Fox and Goose, supervising a delivery in the pub carpark. The sleeves of his denim shirt were rolled up and his face looked hot. Mandy hurried over. 'Mr Hardy!' she called. She thought maybe he had seen something.

Mr Hardy put down the crate of beer that he was carrying and smiled, wiping the sweat away from his forehead. 'Hello, Mandy. What can I do for you?'

'Did you seen Jean get off the bus just now? Jean Knox, from the surgery?' Mandy asked urgently.

Mr Hardy thought for a moment. 'Yes, I think I did. A couple of people got off and I'm sure Jean was one of them.'

'Which way did she go?'

Mr Hardy frowned and then shrugged helplessly. 'Sorry. I didn't notice. Is it important?'

'Never mind,' Mandy sighed. 'Thanks anyway.' She went back to James. 'No luck,' she said.

'Jean had lots of shopping with her,' James pointed out. 'I bet she's just gone back to her house.'

'Of course!' Mandy said. Jean would be bound to go home with all those shopping bags. She jumped on her bike. 'Let's go!'

They set off for Jean's cottage, but when they

got there and knocked on the door there was no reply. Disappointment flooded through Mandy. She had been sure that Jean would be there. 'Where can she be?' she asked, pushing back her hair from her damp forehead.

James looked mystified. 'I don't know.'

Mandy was hot and tired, but she wasn't going to give up on finding Jean and the chinchilla just yet. 'Let's go to my house. Maybe Mum or Dad will have some ideas.'

They got back on to their bikes. 'I wonder who the chinchilla belongs to?' Mandy said as they set off for Animal Ark.

'Are you *sure* it was a chinchilla?' James asked. 'I mean it could have been a rat or something.' He grinned. 'Imagine Jean's face if she takes out her shopping and a rat pops out!'

Despite the funny picture that James's words conjured up, Mandy just shook her head. 'It definitely wasn't a rat!' she said. 'It was too fluffy and it had big oval ears and a bushy tail.' The more she thought about the animal, the more certain she became that it was a chinchilla.

'I guess it does *sound* like a chinchilla,' James said cautiously.

'It *was* a chinchilla!' Mandy insisted.

'Well, whatever it is, it's now in one of Jean's bags,' said James. He looked anxiously at Mandy. 'Wherever she is.'

Reaching Animal Ark they sped up the driveway, past the wooden sign that said *Animal Ark – Veterinary Surgery*, and came to a stop by the low modern extension that had been built on to the stone cottage to house Mandy's parents' veterinary practice. Leaving their bikes leaning against the wall, they ran into the waiting-room.

Mandy immediately stopped dead. 'Jean!' she gasped.

Jean was standing by the desk, talking to Emily Hope, Mandy's mum. Hearing the astonishment in Mandy's voice, she looked rather surprised. 'Hello, dear.'

'Have you had a good day at school?' said Mrs Hope with a smile, coming forward to meet them.

But Mandy wasn't listening. 'Stand still, Mum!' she hissed urgently, staring at the shopping bags piled around Jean's feet. 'Don't move!' She spun round to James and spoke in a frantic whisper. 'Quick! Shut the door!'

Almost before the words were out of her mouth, James had carefully shut the door. 'And the windows!' he whispered back.

Moving as swiftly but as quietly as she could, Mandy shut the windows and then closed the door that connected the waiting-room with the rest of the surgery and the house.

Mrs Hope and Jean looked at each other in astonishment. 'What on earth is going on?' Mrs Hope asked, her green eyes wide. 'Mandy, why are you whispering?'

'Shh!' Mandy said in alarm. Still speaking in a whisper she hurriedly explained. 'There's a chinchilla in one of Jean's bags. I saw it jump in when Jean was getting on the bus.'

'We've been trying to catch up with her ever since the bus left Walton,' James added.

Jean looked as if she could hardly believe her ears. 'A chinchilla?' she exclaimed in a high-pitched voice.

'Sshh!' Mandy said desperately.

Jean dropped her voice. 'There's a chinchilla?' she whispered incredulously. 'In one of my bags?'

Mandy nodded. 'It ran along the pavement and jumped in and then I saw it again when you were sitting on the back seat. It poked its head out.'

'Are you sure, Mandy?' Mrs Hope said in a low voice.

'Yes! Positive!' Mandy hissed.

Everyone looked at the mass of bags on the floor. 'Well, I suppose we'd better have a look,' Mrs Hope said, frowning. She looked at Jean. 'You don't mind if we look in your bags, do you?'

'No, go ahead,' Jean said, peering rather cautiously at the bags on the floor.

Mrs Hope, Mandy and James knelt down. 'Be careful,' Mrs Hope warned, tucking her long red hair behind her ears. 'Chinchillas tend to bite when they're scared.'

Mandy reached for a bag and carefully started to take things out – sun cream, hairspray, some rose-scented body lotion, talc – but no chinchilla. 'It's not in this one,' she whispered.

Jean watched rather nervously from a distance. 'Oh dear, I hope it's all right.'

'Are you *sure* it was a chinchilla, Mandy?' Mrs Hope said, emptying the last of the contents out of the bag in front of her and turning it inside out.

'Yes.' Mandy hesitated for a moment. 'Well, as sure as I could be,' she admitted. 'It was like the one that someone brought in here once, but it was light brown, not grey.'

'Some of them are beige,' confirmed Mrs Hope. 'But they're not very common.'

'I'm *sure* it was a chinchilla, Mum,' Mandy said as she reached the bottom of her second bag. She looked into the centre. There was just one bag left. It stood by itself in the middle of the floor. 'It must be in there!' she breathed.

'Quietly now,' said Mrs Hope, easing the bag

over towards her. She slowly began to remove the contents. Mandy, James and Jean leaned forward. The air was tense with expectancy. *What* was going to come out?

'A necklace, a scarf, some tights,' muttered Mrs Hope under her breath as she took out the contents. 'A dress.' She pulled out a flowery dress and looked into the bag. 'And that's it.' She sat back on her heels and looked at them. 'No chinchilla.'

Mandy saw her mother and Jean exchange glances. 'I saw one, I really did!' she exclaimed. 'It must have escaped before we got here!'

'Well, I came straight here from the bus stop,' Jean said. 'I'm sure I would have noticed if it had jumped out of my bag on the way.'

'So it's got to be either here or on the bus,' said James logically.

'It might have got out of the bag while you were talking,' Mandy said to her mum and Jean. She looked anxiously at the door that led through to the rest of the surgery. 'It could be in the surgery or even have gone through to the house. We've got to find it!'

Mrs Hope glanced at her watch. 'I suppose

we've got time to have a quick look before surgery starts,' she said.

'We'll search the house!' Mandy said. 'Come on, James!'

Leaving Mrs Hope and Jean to search the surgery, they hurried through to the cottage. They started downstairs, creeping through all the rooms, looking under chairs, in the wastepaper baskets, in the coal scuttle, up the chimney and under the sofa, but there was no sign of a chinchilla.

'What about upstairs?' James whispered at last.

They tiptoed over to the staircase. They were halfway up when a sudden loud hammering noise from the bathroom made them both jump.

'What's that?' James asked in surprise.

'The decorators!' Mandy groaned in dismay. 'We're having a new bathroom fitted. If the chinchilla's gone upstairs it's going to be terrified by now!'

They hurried up the stairs and quickly searched the bedrooms, but there was no sign of the chinchilla. The noise of hammering still continued in the background.

'Maybe the decorators have seen it,' James suggested.

The bathroom door was open. Two men wearing paint-stained dungarees were working inside. One was painting whilst the other was fixing new pine panels on to the side of the bath.

'Hi,' Mandy said. They stopped working and looked round. 'Um . . . you haven't seen a chinchilla, have you?' she said.

The men looked at her rather blankly.

'It's a small furry creature,' she said, feeling her face go hot and red. 'Beige fur, large ears, fluffy tail . . .'

'Oh, a chihuahua,' said the man with the paint brush in his hand, a look of understanding crossing his face.

'No, not a chihuahua,' said Mandy. 'That's a dog.'

'Yes I know,' said the man. 'My granny used to have one. Funny little thing it was too.' He looked at the other man. 'Well, Joe, seen any chihuahuas round here today?'

'No, can't say that I have,' said Joe. 'Course, one could have snuck in here while we went downstairs for a cuppa.'

'But I'm not looking for a chihuahua,' said Mandy. 'I'm looking for a chinchilla! Have you seen one?'

The first man thought for a moment and then shook his head. 'No.' He grinned at her. 'How about a chimpanzee? We must have seen at least three of those today.'

'Or a chipmunk?' Joe called after her. 'There's been ten of those!'

Mandy gave up and turned away. 'How about a chicken?' they called after her.

'Well, they were a lot of help,' Mandy said, rejoining James.

The hammering started up again. 'Well, I can't see a chinchilla staying up here with all this noise,' James said. 'Come on.'

They went back downstairs. 'Where can it be?' Mandy said, looking round the living-room.

James scratched his head. 'Are you *sure* you saw something?'

'Yes!' Mandy insisted.

Just then the living-room door opened and Mrs Hope came in. 'No luck in the surgery,' she said, running a hand through her hair. She looked rather doubtfully at Mandy. 'Are you absolutely—'

'Yes!' Mandy exclaimed before her mother could finish. She looked round at them both. 'Why won't anyone believe me?' she demanded. 'I saw it get into Jean's bag. It's got to be here somewhere.'

'Well, I'm afraid Jean and I are going to have to stop looking now,' Mrs Hope said. 'It's almost time for surgery. Maybe you should ring the bus company. Someone may have reported seeing it on the bus.'

Mandy's eyes lit up. 'Good idea, Mum! I'll get the phone book!'

Mrs Hope returned to the surgery and Mandy and James leafed through the telephone directory until they found the bus company's number.

Mandy picked up the phone. To her relief, the man who answered, Mr Holms, was interested and helpful, but he told her that there had been no reports of a chinchilla or any other small animal.

'Try ringing again tomorrow,' he said. 'Wait

until lunch-time – we're more likely to have heard something by then.'

Mandy put the phone down.

'No luck?' said James.

She shook her head. 'But he said to try again tomorrow.' She looked round. 'Maybe we should have another look.'

James shuffled his feet. 'I'd better be getting home,' he said rather quickly. 'Blackie will be wanting his walk and Mum will be wondering where I am.'

Mandy followed him to the door. As he got on to his bike, he looked at her anxious face. 'Don't worry,' he said rather awkwardly. 'I'm sure it will turn up.'

Mandy nodded. She had a feeling that he still didn't really believe her. Going slowly back inside, she shut the door and looked round. Whatever James and her mum thought, she *knew* what she had seen. Somewhere, there was a lost and frightened chinchilla. She decided to start searching again.

After going through the whole house twice more, Mandy was finally forced to admit that the chinchilla didn't seem to be hiding at

Animal Ark. *Maybe it got out on the bus, after all,* she thought. She hoped there would be some news when she rang the bus company the next day.

She went upstairs, took out all her animal books and looked through them for information on chinchillas. At last, she found something. It was just a short paragraph next to a photograph:

Chinchilla: member of the rodent family. Commonly grey in colour but shades of brown, black and white also possible. Vegetarian. Can be tamed but easily frightened by loud noises and sudden movements.

Mandy studied the creature in the photograph. It was grey, but in every other way it looked just like the animal that had poked its head out of Jean's bag on the bus that afternoon – the same large ears; the long, twitching whiskers; the bright dark eyes and fluffy coat. It looked so sweet. Mandy's heart twisted as she thought about the chinchilla she had seen. Was it hiding somewhere – lost and scared? Mandy was resolute. Wherever it was, she was determined to find it!

Three

Mandy woke up early the next morning. She'd had a restless night, worrying about the chinchilla.

As she grabbed a piece of toast before morning surgery she glanced at the phone. She was longing to ring the bus company but she knew she should wait until lunch-time. Mandy sighed. It was just so difficult to wait. There might have been a sighting and someone might have reported something already. Her fingers itched to dial the number.

'Are you ready?' Mrs Hope said, buttoning

up her white coat as she came into the kitchen. Swallowing her last mouthful of toast, Mandy nodded. Maybe the daily routine of morning surgery was just what she needed to take her mind off the chinchilla for a while.

Saturday surgery was always busy. Mandy was soon hurrying around: helping Jean as she tried to answer the phone and talk to clients at the same time; fetching worming tablets for her mum; mopping up a puddle made by a puppy on the waiting-room floor. It wasn't hard to stay occupied. There was always something to be done, and Mandy soon managed to push all thoughts of the chinchilla to the back of her mind.

Coming out of the consulting room after helping to hold a rabbit who needed eardrops, Mandy saw one of her school friends sitting with a small cardboard box on her knee. 'Hi, Amy!' she said, hurrying over.

Amy Fenton looked up. 'Hi, Mandy.' She was a year younger than Mandy, the same age as James.

Mandy looked anxiously at the cardboard box. 'Is something the matter with Minnie?' Minnie was Amy's white mouse. Amy had owned her since she was eight years old.

Amy nodded. 'She's got a lump.'

Mandy felt her heart sink. She knew that lumps could be serious.

'It's been getting bigger and bigger.' Amy swallowed. 'She's three years old now, you know, Mandy. And that's quite old for a mouse.'

Mandy's eyes were wide with sympathy. 'It'll be OK,' she said.

Amy smiled faintly at her. 'I hope so.'

Just then, Mrs Hope came through. 'Amy, do you want to come in now?' she said.

Amy stood up and looked at Mandy. 'Are you coming?'

Mandy glanced at her mum, who nodded.

Once in the consulting room, Amy explained the problem. Mrs Hope took Minnie out of her box. 'It's under her front leg,' Amy said.

Mrs Hope gently held the little white mouse in her hands and inspected the lump. It was large and swung slightly from side to side. Mandy bit her lip. She was sure that it looked serious.

Mrs Hope didn't need long to make her

diagnosis. 'It's a mammary tumour, Amy,' she said. 'It may be malignant or it may be benign. If it's benign then it will do no harm although it may keep growing and start to hinder Minnie's movement in the end.'

'And if it's malignant?' whispered Amy.

'Then I'm afraid that means it will spread, Amy,' Mrs Hope said gently.

'And she'll die?' Amy asked, her voice catching.

Mrs Hope nodded. 'The cancer will eventually spread to other parts of Minnie's body.'

Mandy felt the tears spring to her eyes. 'What can you do, Mum?' she asked, looking at Minnie lying so quietly on her mother's hand.

'Well, we could remove it,' Mrs Hope said. 'And if we did, we would send the lump off to the lab for analysis.' She shook her head slightly. 'But Minnie's an old mouse now. In a case like this I would generally just advise to leave the lump alone rather than put her through the trauma of an operation.'

Mandy looked anxiously at her friend. Amy's eyes were brimming with tears. 'But you *could* operate?' she said to Mrs Hope.

Mrs Hope nodded. 'We could.' Her eyes gently searched Amy's face. 'It's up to you. What do you want us to do?'

Mandy waited breathlessly for Amy's answer.

'Well . . . um . . .' Amy struggled for words, her voice low. 'Will you operate, please?' Mandy felt a rush of relief. She knew there was a risk involved in the operation *and* that there was no guarantee that her mum could do anything, but at least this way there was a chance that Minnie might be all right.

Mrs Hope nodded. 'But don't get your hopes up. I'm afraid that mammary tumours in mice are generally malignant.'

Amy nodded. She didn't seem to trust herself to speak.

Now that a decision had been made, Mrs Hope became practical and brisk. 'Right, we'll keep her in now, then,' she said. 'We don't normally operate on Saturday, but the sooner the better in this case. I'll want her to stay in tonight for observation but you can collect her tomorrow morning. I'll give your mum a ring now, then we'll call you after the operation to tell you how it went.' She turned to Mandy. 'Mandy will you take Amy and Minnie through to the residential unit, please?'

Forcing back her own tears, Mandy tried to echo her mum's professional efficiency. 'Come on,' she said, putting an arm round her friend's shoulders. 'Let's go and get Minnie settled in.'

In the residential unit, they put Minnie in a cage. 'It'll be all right,' Amy whispered to the little mouse. 'You'll see.' Now she was out of the consulting room, she let the tears trickle freely down her cheeks.

A hard lump pressed painfully against Mandy's throat. 'Don't worry,' she said. 'I'll look after her.'

Amy brushed the back of her hand across her face. 'Thanks.' She took one long look at the cage. 'Bye, Minnie.' Sniffing, she turned and left.

Mandy swallowed hard as the door shut behind Amy. *It isn't fair*, she thought – she hated seeing any animal being really ill, but somehow it was always worse when it was an animal belonging to one of her friends.

* * *

After morning surgery finished, Mrs Hope and Simon, the practice nurse, got ready to operate. Mandy was allowed to watch. Her heart beat fast as she carried Minnie through from the residential wing.

When she was satisfied that the anaesthetic was working, Mrs Hope carefully removed the lump. 'It doesn't look too bad,' Mrs Hope said, as the round, smooth lump popped on to a dish Simon was holding. 'Malignant tumours normally have rougher edges than this,' she told Mandy.

'So it might be benign?' Mandy asked eagerly.

'It might be,' said Mrs Hope. 'But don't get your hopes up just yet. We'll have to wait for the lab results to be sure.'

It only took a few stitches to close the wound. 'There, all done,' said Emily Hope, tying off the last stitch. She looked at Mandy. 'Now, we just have to wait and see.'

After Mandy had phoned Amy to say that Minnie's operation had all gone according to plan, she rang the bus company and asked to speak to Mr Holms – the man she had spoken to the day before. She waited for him to come to the phone. Butterflies were fluttering in her stomach. Would there be any news on the chinchilla?

'Martin Holms here,' said a friendly voice.

'Hi,' Mandy said quickly. 'It's Mandy Hope. I spoke to you yesterday about a missing chinchilla. I was wondering if there was any news?' She waited on tenterhooks for his answer.

'Sorry, love,' Mr Holms said. 'Nothing's been reported yet.'

Mandy's heart sank. 'Oh.'

Mr Holms seemed to hear the disappointment in her voice. 'Look, why don't you make a few posters? We'll put them up in the buses that go from Walton to Welford for you. Someone might have seen something and not reported it.'

'OK!' Mandy said eagerly. 'Thanks!'

'Just drop them in at the depot when they're done,' Mr Holms said.

As soon as Mandy put the phone down she got started on making the posters. She decided to copy the picture of the chinchilla from her animal book on to the posters, so that people who saw the posters would know what sort of animal to look out for. After she had finished, she wrote 'Information wanted!' in big letters at the top of each poster, and underneath the picture she wrote the details of the missing chinchilla and Animal Ark's telephone number.

'Hi!' James said, poking his head round the kitchen door just as she was finishing them. 'Your mum said you were in here.' He looked curiously at the paper and pens on the tables. 'What are you doing?'

Mandy explained. 'I've got to take these posters to the bus depot.' She quickly wrote the phone number on the last one and stood up. 'They're all finished. Shall we go there now?'

They cycled over to the bus depot with the posters in Mandy's bag and left the posters with Mr Holms.

'They'll by put up tomorrow,' he said. He looked at the drawing of the chinchilla. 'They're sweet little things, aren't they?'

Mandy nodded. 'And we need to find this one as quickly as possible.'

'Well, let's hope you get some response then,'

Mr Holms said. 'I'll give you a ring if I hear anything.'

Mandy smiled at him gratefully. 'Thanks!'

She and James cycled slowly back to Animal Ark, the sun baking down on their bare arms and legs.

'I need an ice lolly,' said Mandy, wiping her damp forehead as she got off her bike. 'Do you want one?'

'Definitely!' James said, following her into the house. Mandy was just handing him an ice lolly from the freezer when the kitchen door opened and the decorators came in.

'What animal are you looking for now?' one of them said, looking at the open freezer door. 'A polar bear?' He grinned. 'Is your mum around, love? The bathroom's done.'

'I'll just get her,' Mandy said, glad to escape from their teasing. She hurried into the surgery and found Mrs Hope looking through some paperwork. 'The bathroom's ready, Mum,' she said. 'The decorators want you.'

'Oh great!' Emily Hope said, jumping to her feet. She came through to the kitchen and went upstairs with the decorators to look at the new bathroom. Mandy and James followed.

'It's perfect!' said Mrs Hope happily. Mandy looked round. She had to admit that it was a big improvement. The sink and bath gleamed snowy-white, the new chunky chrome taps shone and the bath had been panelled in honey-coloured pine. A new wooden cupboard had been fixed to the wall and a matching mirror hung over the sink.

Mrs Hope started talking to the decorators about little details and, soon bored, Mandy and James wandered downstairs again. 'Do you want to come and see Minnie?' Mandy asked, sucking the last of her rapidly-melting ice lolly off its stick. She had told James about Minnie's operation on the way back from the bus depot.

James nodded and they went through to the residential unit. Minnie was the only animal there. They found her sniffing round the walls of her cage. 'Minnie!' Mandy called softly, crouching down beside the bars of the cage. Minnie looked round and trotted over; sitting back on her hind legs she squeaked loudly.

Mandy grinned. 'Same old Minnie!'

James tickled Minnie's nose through the bars

of the cage. 'Do you remember when we were at primary school and Minnie was in the school play?'

Mandy nodded. 'It seems ages ago, doesn't it?' She watched as Minnie scampered over to her food bowl. The little mouse was slower than she used to be, and her coat looked thinner, but her eyes were still bright. Mandy swallowed hard. *Oh Minnie*, she prayed. *Please be all right.*

It was a hot night and when Mandy went to bed she threw back her duvet and lay on her sheet.

Turning off the light, she tried to find a comfortable position. Her mind was racing. One minute she thought about Minnie, the next about the missing chinchilla. White pointed face. Brown fluffy face. One after the other. At last she drifted off.

Some time later she woke up. Looking at the luminous hands of her clock, she saw that it was two o'clock in the morning. Feeling hot and sticky she jumped out of bed, went over to the window and threw it open. Cool night air flooded in. She breathed in deeply, enjoying the delicious feeling of it on her warm skin.

Squeak! Squeak!

Mandy stiffened. What was that?

Squeak! Squeak!

There it was again. Faint, but high-pitched.

Mandy relaxed. *Of course*, she thought, *Minnie!* She looked downwards; the noise must be carrying up to her window from the residential unit. She smiled to herself. Minnie might be an old mouse but she certainly made a lot of noise still!

Going back to bed she lay down. Her room

was cooler now and she soon started drifting off to sleep.

Squeak! Squeak!

Half asleep, Mandy frowned slightly. It was strange that she could still hear Minnie so clearly from her bed.

Squeak! Squeak!

Mandy gave up puzzling about it. Turning over, she went to sleep.

'Come through, Amy,' Mrs Hope said, showing her into the residential wing. It was nine o'clock the next morning and Amy had arrived just as Animal Ark was opening for morning surgery.

'Minnie's looking fine,' Mandy said comfortingly. 'She squeaked a bit last night, though. She must have been missing you.'

Amy smiled. 'I missed her too.' As soon as they reached the residential wing she hurried up to the cage. Minnie scampered over to the bars. Amy turned to Mrs Hope. 'Can I take her out?'

Mrs Hope smiled. 'Of course.'

As soon as Amy reached into the cage, Minnie hopped on to her hand. 'She shouldn't need any special care,' Mrs Hope said. 'Bring her back in a week and I'll take the stitches out then. And when I get the results of the biopsy I'll give you a ring straight away.'

Amy cuddled Minnie close to her chest. 'Mandy said it would take about a week,' she said.

'That's right,' Emily Hope said. 'Now, try not to worry too much in the meantime.'

'Thanks, Mrs Hope,' Amy replied, putting Minnie carefully into her travelling box. 'Mum said, can you send the bill to our house?'

Mrs Hope nodded. 'I'll sort that out this week.'

Mandy opened the door for Amy.

'Thanks,' Amy said gratefully. 'Bye. See you soon.'

As she went out, Mrs Hope came over and put her arm round Mandy's shoulders. Together they watched Amy walk down the drive, carefully cradling Minnie's box in her arms.

To Mandy's disappointment, there were no phone calls about the chinchilla that day. *Still*, she thought to herself as she got ready for bed, *it is Sunday. Maybe people haven't seen the posters yet.*

It was warm again that night. Mandy slept restlessly and woke at four o'clock in the morning. Her mouth felt dry. She was just deciding whether she could be bothered to get a drink when she heard a noise:

Squeak! Squeak!

Mandy sat bolt upright. That squeaking noise again! She frowned. It couldn't be Minnie this time. So what was it?

Sitting as still as she could, she listened hard. For a while she heard nothing but then it started again:

Squeak! Squeak!

It sounded like an animal in distress. Quickly pushing back her sheet, Mandy got up. This was something she had to investigate!

Four

Mandy opened her bedroom door and listened hard. Everywhere was quiet. Maybe the noise was coming from downstairs. She crept to the top of the staircase.

Feeling for the banisters, she tiptoed cautiously down. There was still no squeaking noise. Putting the lights on, she looked round, but there was no sign of anything unusual. She checked the living-room and the kitchen and the study. Nothing. *But something had to have been making that noise*, she thought. *What was it?*

Turning the lights back off, she crept back up the stairs.

Squeak! Squeak!

Mandy froze, one foot poised in midair. There it was again! She wondered whether the noise had come from upstairs or downstairs. It was hard to tell. She stood still for a while, listening, but there were no further clues. Taking careful steps, she carried on up the stairs and went into the bathroom and looked around in there, but everything seemed perfectly normal.

She rubbed her head and sat down heavily on the side of the bath. She was beginning to wonder if she was hearing things!

SQUEAK!

Mandy almost jumped out of her skin. She stared down at the bath beneath her.

SQUEAK! SQUEAK!

Mandy leaped to her feet. It was unmistakable. The noise was coming from underneath her. It was coming from *behind* the pine panelling that the decorators had fixed on to the side of the bath!

Mandy didn't stop to think. She flew along the landing to her parents' room. 'Mum! Dad!

she gasped, bursting in through the door.

Mr and Mrs Hope both sat up in alarm. 'What is it, Mandy?' Mrs Hope said sleepily, switching the light on. 'Are you all right?'

'There's an animal in the bathroom!' Mandy cried. 'It's trapped behind the bath! Quick! You've got to help!'

Within seconds, Mr and Mrs Hope were pulling on their dressing-gowns and hurrying along the corridor. 'I heard it squeak when I sat down on the bath,' Mandy said. As if on cue, as they pushed the bathroom door open the animal behind the bath made a loud squeaking noise again.

'There it is!' Mandy exclaimed.

Mr Hope pushed a hand through his dark hair. 'I guess we'd better take the panels off,' he said, kneeling down to examine them. 'It doesn't look too difficult. I'll go and get a screwdriver.' He hurried downstairs.

'I wonder what it can be?' Mrs Hope wondered, crouching down and putting her ear to the panelling. 'It sounds too loud for a mouse.' She pushed her long hair back behind her ears. 'Maybe it's a rat?'

But Mandy had another idea. 'It could be the chinchilla,' she said.

'You said the decorators didn't see anything,' Mrs Hope pointed out.

'Maybe they just didn't notice it,' Mandy suggested. 'It could have come in here when they were having a tea break.'

But her mum didn't look convinced.

'Right then,' said Adam Hope, returning quickly with a screwdriver, a cardboard rodent-carrier from the surgery and two pairs of leather gloves. He shut the door and handed the gloves to Mrs Hope and Mandy. 'It may run out as soon as I take the side off. I want you two to try and catch it – whatever it is.'

Mandy crouched down eagerly. Off came one panel and then the next and then the next. She waited anxiously, every muscle tense, wondering what was going to come running out.

At last, the whole of the side of the bath was taken off, but there was no sign of the animal. Mandy and her parents peered under the bath. There was nothing there.

'Where's it gone?' said Mandy in astonishment.

Mr Hope pointed to a hole in one of the floorboards. 'Look! It's got an escape route.' He saw Mandy's mouth open. 'No, Mandy,' he said, sitting back firmly. 'I am *not* taking the floorboards up.'

'But, Dad!' Mandy protested. 'We can't leave it down there.' She thought of the distressed squeak. 'It's probably terrified!'

'Why don't you go and get some rabbit pellets from downstairs, Mandy?' Mrs Hope suggested. 'It must be hungry. If we leave some on the floor, maybe it will come out when we've gone.'

'But then it will escape!' said Mandy.

'Not if we keep the bathroom door shut,' her mum said. 'It will still be in here in the morning and we can catch it then.'

Mandy quickly realised the sense in the plan. She hurried downstairs, returning a few minutes later with some rabbit pellets and a small dish which she filled with water from the sink. She laid the dish and the pellets down carefully on the floor in front of the bath and looked at the floorboards.

'Come on,' Mrs Hope said gently, putting a hand on her shoulder. 'Back to bed!'

They all left the bathroom and, shutting the door carefully behind them, went back to their rooms. Mandy got into bed but she couldn't sleep. She lay awake wondering what was happening in the bathroom. Had the animal come out? Was it eating the food? She hugged her arms round her chest. What would they find in the morning?

Mandy woke up at six-thirty. She crept to the bathroom, put on one of the pairs of leather gloves that her dad had left on the landing, and cautiously inched the bathroom door open. She peeped in through the crack. There was nothing to be seen.

Opening the door just wide enough to slip through, she dashed in and closed it quickly behind her. She wasn't going to risk the animal escaping!

She looked round. The food had gone. *So the animal must have been out*, she thought. She looked round the bathroom, half expecting to see something furry watching her from a corner, but there was nothing. Crouching down, she peered under the bath. The animal must have run back under the floorboards again.

Leaning forwards, Mandy put her ear to the floor. She listened hard. At first there was nothing but then she heard a faint gnawing sound. So it *was* still under there!

She sat back on her heels. The poor creature must have been terrified when it found itself nailed up behind the bath. It must be traumatised, she thought. How were they ever going to persuade it to come out and be caught?

Just then there was a gentle knock on the bathroom door. Mandy got to her feet and opened it a crack. It was her mother. 'Any luck?' Mrs Hope asked. She was wearing a white towelling dressing-gown and her long red hair spilled down round her shoulders.

Mandy shook her head.

'Well, I was going to have a bath,' said Mrs Hope.

'You can't, Mum!' Mandy exclaimed. 'It will frighten the creature more than ever.'

'But . . .'

'Please, Mum,' Mandy begged. 'Have a shower instead.'

Mrs Hope sighed. 'So much for having a new bathroom,' she said drily. But she gave in and went downstairs to the shower room.

After breakfast, Mandy rang James and explained about the animal. 'I'm going to watch the bathroom all day,' she said, 'and see if it comes out.'

James immediately promised to come round and help. He cycled over and joined Mandy in the bathroom a little while later. 'If we sit quietly enough it might just appear,' Mandy said. She pointed to a handful of raisins, a piece of apple and a few sunflower seeds on the floor. 'I thought some treats might tempt it.'

'Good idea,' whispered James, sitting down. 'But how did you know what food to put down?'

'Well, I put down treats that a rodent would like,' she explained. 'From the way it was squeaking it's got to be some sort of rodent.'

'Like a rat or a mouse,' James said.

'Or a chinchilla!' Mandy replied.

Just like her mum, James didn't look so sure.

They waited all morning but nothing happened. 'Maybe we should put the treats a bit nearer the hole,' James suggested.

Mandy nodded. As quietly as she could, she took a few raisins out of the dish and scattered them near to the hole in the floorboards.

They settled down again. After about twenty minutes, James glanced at his watch. 'I'm hungry,' he said. 'What are we going to do about lunch?'

Mandy grabbed his arm. 'Look!' she whispered, staring under the bath. James followed her gaze. A pair of long pale whiskers were poking out. Sitting perfectly still, they watched as two tiny pink paws and a beige-coloured head appeared. Two dark eyes peeped out. Two large round ears twitched.

'Wow!' whispered James, staring in amazement.

'It *is* the chinchilla!' Mandy breathed in delight.

Seeing the raisins, the chinchilla hopped cautiously out of the hole and crept towards them. Mandy was shocked by its appearance. Its previously fluffy beige coat was now matted and separated. Looking round nervously, it seized a raisin in its front paws and started to nibble it with swift sideways movements of its head.

Mandy and James exchanged looks but neither of them dared to do anything. Mandy had no doubt that if they made the slightest movement towards it, the chinchilla would be back under the floorboards in a flash. She looked over to the hole. What were they going to do? They needed to block off its escape route somehow. Maybe she could throw something over the hole – but would she be quick enough? She doubted it.

James shifted his position slightly. The chinchilla's head shot up. It stared at them, its eyes wide for a moment, but then to Mandy's relief it seemed to decide that it was safe to carry on eating. With a quick, jerky movement it started nibbling at the raisin again. Mandy breathed out slowly and exchanged a thankful look with James. Maybe it would get used to them, she thought. Maybe if they just sat very, very quietly . . .

The bathroom door suddenly opened. 'Here's some lunch,' Mrs Hope said cheerfully, appearing with a tray of sandwiches and crisps.

Mandy gasped in dismay. The chinchilla froze

for a second and then, dropping the raisin, streaked towards the door, its ears flat back, its tail flying out behind it.

'Oh!' cried Mrs Hope, almost dropping the tray as the chinchilla flew past her.

'Quick!' Mandy cried, leaping to her feet. 'We can't let it get away!'

The chinchilla dashed along the corridor and down the stairs with Mandy and James in close pursuit. They reached the living-room door just in time to see it racing towards the large stone fireplace.

'Oh no!' Mandy gasped, realising where it was heading.

With one agile bound, the chinchilla leaped up the chimney. Mandy and James looked at each other.

What were they going to do *now*?

Five

Mrs Hope, Mandy and James all looked at the chimney. 'Oh dear,' said Mrs Hope, running a hand over her forehead. 'I didn't realise that it had come out from under the floorboards. I'm sorry.'

'Well, at least it hasn't escaped outside,' Mandy said, trying as hard as she could to look on the bright side. 'And at least we know it's a chinchilla now.'

Emily Hope sighed. 'Yes, you were right, love. It certainly *is* a chinchilla.'

'It's going to be a very *sooty* chinchilla,' said

James, investigating the fireplace, where several piles of fine black soot had fallen on to the stone hearth.

Mandy joined him and, crouching down, tried peering up the chimney to see if she could see anything. But it was too dark. 'How are we going to get it out?' she asked her mum.

'I'll get your father,' Mrs Hope decided. 'He knows a bit more than I do about chinchillas. A school-friend of his used to breed them.' She hurried through the door.

Mandy sat back on her heels. 'Poor little thing,' she said. 'It must be so frightened.'

James was still looking as if he could hardly believe his eyes. 'I wonder who it belongs to?' he said.

Mandy thought for a moment. 'Well, it must be someone in Walton because that's where I saw it first,' she said. 'Maybe we could put an advert in the "Lost and Found" section of the *Walton Gazette*.'

'Good idea,' James agreed. 'We can ring the paper later.'

'But first, we've got to get it down,' Mandy said.

James nodded. 'It didn't look in very good condition,' he said with concern. 'I hope your dad can think of something.'

But when Mr Hope came through from the surgery he had no ideas. He stood on the rug and scratched at his beard. 'It's not going to be easy. I think the only thing we can do is leave some food out,' he said, 'and hope that as it calms down it will come out. Poking around in the chimney will only frighten it more.'

Mandy scrambled to her feet. 'What sort of food does it need?' she asked.

'Chinchillas are usually fed on special chinchilla pellets,' Mr Hope said. 'They have quite sensitive digestive systems, so you have to be careful what you give them.'

James looked at Mandy. 'Maybe the pet shop will have some,' he suggested.

Mr Hope nodded. 'If they haven't, I'm sure they can get something in. In the meantime, rabbit pellets should be OK. It will also need some clean water in a dish.'

'What about treats?' Mandy asked. 'If we put some treats out it might come down.'

Adam Hope nodded. 'You can certainly try.

Chinchillas like the same sort of things rats and mice do – raisins and sunflower seeds.' He looked at them warningly. 'But too many treats will upset its digestion – so just use a few.'

Mandy nodded. 'OK. So how long do you think it will be before it comes out?'

Mr Hope looked at the chimney, a concerned frown on his face. 'Once frightened, chinchillas can take quite a long time to calm down. They're sensitive creatures and really don't react well to new or stressful situations.'

'Then I think the best thing we can do now is to leave the poor thing in peace and quiet,' Mrs Hope said briskly. 'Why don't you go and get some food for it, Mandy, and then we'll all leave it alone for a bit?'

Mandy nodded in agreement and went with James to put some rabbit pellets in a dish and fill up a bowl with fresh water. They put the water and food on the rug by the fireplace and set out two raisins next to the food bowl. Then, shutting the door carefully, they went through to the kitchen.

Mrs Hope had brought the tray of sandwiches down from the bathroom. 'How about some lunch?' she said as they came through. James nodded eagerly and sat down at the table, but Mandy's mind was too full of the chinchilla to think about food.

'Come on, love,' Mrs Hope said, seeing her expression. 'You're not going to help the chinchilla by starving yourself. There's nothing you can do at the moment but wait.' Mandy sighed but she could see that her mum was right. She sat down next to James.

'They do look good!' Mandy's dad said, reaching over and helping himself to two of the sandwiches as Emily Hope put the tray down on the table.

Mrs Hope slapped his wrist. 'They're supposed to be for Mandy and James!' she exclaimed.

'It's all right, Dad,' said Mandy, looking at the overflowing plate of sandwiches. 'There are loads. We'll never eat them all.'

'That's what I like to hear,' said Mr Hope. He fetched a plate and sat down happily beside her. 'Come on, James. Tuck in!'

'Are you going to have some, Mum?' Mandy asked.

Mrs Hope shook her head. 'I'll make myself some later. Right now, I'm going to have a bath.'

Mandy stared at her in surprise. 'A bath? But it's lunch-time!'

'It's also the first time I've had the luxury of having my new bathroom all to myself,' Mrs Hope said. 'I'm going to have a good long soak.' She stopped by the door, her green eyes twinkling slightly. 'Unless, of course, you've got some other reason why I shouldn't? A canary in the cupboard, maybe?'

Mandy managed a grin. 'No, a chinchilla up the chimney's enough. Enjoy your bath.'

'I intend to,' Mrs Hope said firmly as she disappeared up the stairs.

Munching on a cheese sandwich, Mr Hope gave them some advice on the chinchilla. 'If you're watching for it to come out from the chimney you want to avoid making any sudden movement or noise,' he said. 'Don't make a "shushing" sound at them or let your clothes swish; anything that sounds even remotely like the hissing of a snake terrifies them.'

'It certainly seems quite nervous. But people do keep them as pets, don't they?' asked James, reaching for another sandwich.

'Oh yes, they can be very tame and affectionate once they get to know you,' Mr Hope replied. 'They just tend to be a bit nervous in the beginning. My friend had four chinchillas. One of them used to ride round on his shoulder and beg for a titbit, and another would squeak on command.'

'What colour were your friend's chinchillas, Dad?' Mandy asked.

'Grey,' Mr Hope said.

'This one's beige,' said Mandy. 'Oh, and its coat has got really matted. It was fluffy when I first saw it, but now it looks dreadful.'

'Chinchillas need regular dust-baths to keep their fur in good condition,' Mr Hope explained. 'It gets rid of the excess moisture and grease in their thick fur.'

'Dust-baths?' James said. 'Doesn't that make them more dirty?'

Mr Hope grinned. 'Chinchilla owners don't use real dust. They usually use a special kind of very fine, powdery Spanish sand called sepiolita.'

'We should get some,' James said to Mandy.

'I'm going to ring up the pet shop,' Mandy decided. 'I'll see if they've got some chinchilla pellets and some sepiolita. We can leave it out in a dish for it to bathe in.'

'One of Mum's bread tins should do,' Mr Hope said. 'It needs to be a container with fairly high sides, otherwise all the sand will fly out.'

But when Mandy rang the pet shop, Geoff told her that he didn't keep chinchilla supplies in stock. 'I can get them from York for you,' he explained. 'But there isn't a regular demand so I just order them when needed. They'll take two days to come in.'

Mandy decided that was better than nothing. 'OK. Can you order us some, please?' she said. She thought about the chinchilla's matted coat. Maybe Geoff would know of something else they could use in the meantime. 'Do you know if there is anything else that we can use instead of sepiolita until then?' she asked hopefully.

'Sorry,' Geoff said. 'We don't keep chinchillas, so I'm not really that clued up on them.'

'Never mind,' said Mandy. 'Thanks anyway.' She put the phone down.

'Any luck?' Mr Hope asked.

'Geoff doesn't have anything in stock,' Mandy said. 'He's going to order us some pellets and sepiolita but it will take two days.' She thought of the pitiful state of the chinchilla up the chimney. 'But the chinchilla needs a dust-bath now. What are we going to do?'

'Isn't there anything else we can use?' said James. 'What about normal sand?'

Mr Hope shook his head. 'No, it's too coarse, I'm afraid.' He frowned thoughtfully. 'I'm sure there is something else you *can* use though. Let me think. It's something that's quite easy to get hold of.' Mandy and James waited anxiously. But in the end Mr Hope shook his head. 'Sorry,' he said. 'I can't remember what it is.'

Just then the door opened and Mrs Hope came in. Her hair was tied back and on her face she had a thick, muddy face-mask.

'Very attractive, Mum!' Mandy grinned.

'You can be quiet, Mandy Hope,' her mother said, picking up her book from the side. 'This may look silly but I'm enjoying myself!'

'That's it!' Mr Hope exclaimed suddenly. 'Fuller's earth!'

They all turned and looked at him. He was staring at Mrs Hope's face.

'Dad?' Mandy said.

'Fuller's earth!' Mr Hope repeated, looking round at them triumphantly. 'It's used in face-masks *and* you can use it for chinchillas' dust-baths! You can get it from chemists' shops.'

'Brilliant!' Mandy said, jumping to her feet.

'Will the chemist in Walton have some?' James asked, hastily swallowing the last of his sandwich.

Mr Hope nodded. 'Just ask at the counter.' He reached into his pocket and handed Mandy some money. 'Here,' he said. 'And you can use the change to pay for the chinchilla pellets and sepiolita later in the week.'

'Thanks, Dad!' Mandy said, her eyes shining. 'Come on, James! Let's go!'

Mandy and James came out of the chemist's with a heavy bag of fine white powder. 'It looks a bit like talc,' James said, investigating it.

'Let's hope the chinchilla likes it,' Mandy said. She hoped they would see the chinchilla having a bath.

'Do you think we should go to the library?' James suggested as they picked up their bikes. 'They might have some books on chinchillas.'

'OK,' Mandy agreed.

They already knew where the pet section was in the library. Searching among all the books on rabbits, guinea-pigs, rats and mice they found a slim book called *An Owner's Guide to Chinchillas*.

Mandy took it off the shelf and opened it. It had lots of photos of chinchillas inside.

'Aren't they fluffy?' said James, peering over her shoulder.

'Their fur is used for coats.' A shiver ran down Mandy's spine as she read out loud the words next to the pictures on the introductory page. She hated the thought of animals being made into coats. She didn't understand how people could bear to wear fur. Didn't they realise that the coats looked better on the animals than on themselves?

'Don't think about it,' James advised. He turned the page. Chapter One was called *Care of the Chinchilla*. 'Look, it says here about the food chinchillas need and the treats they like,' he pointed out. 'Your dad was right, sunflower seeds and raisins *are* their favourites.'

Mandy read down to the bottom of the page. 'It also says that they hate changes and shocks.' She read a few lines out loud. ' "Chinchillas are usually healthy and robust animals, however they can be easily upset by changes in their routine or surroundings. Sudden changes may result in ill health." ' Her voice died away as she thought about the poor little chinchilla up the chimney. It had experienced lots of changes in the last few days. What if it became ill?

'It'll be all right,' James said comfortingly, seeing the expression on her face. 'It *will* come out soon and then we'll catch it. You'll see.'

Mandy nodded but she still felt worried. A stressed chinchilla was not a healthy chinchilla, according to the book. They had to try to get it down from the chimney as soon as possible. 'Come on,' she said, closing the book. 'Let's take this out and get back to Animal Ark.'

They cycled quickly back to Welford. When they got back to Animal Ark they got out one of Mrs Hope's rectangular bread tins. 'How much should I put in?' James asked, picking up the bag of fuller's earth.

'Hang on, I'll go and ask Dad.' Mandy hurried into the surgery to find her dad and came back with the answer. 'About five centimetres.' As James carefully poured the fuller's earth into the bread tin, Mandy collected a few more raisins from the cupboard. 'Are you ready?' she asked. James nodded.

Quietly opening the living-room door, they crept inside. There was no sign of the chinchilla. Moving as silently as they could, they placed the dust-bath next to the bowl of rabbit pellets.

'The raisins I left out earlier have gone,' Mandy whispered to James. 'It must have been down from the chimney.'

James pointed to a few tiny black paw prints on the rug. 'Look. You can see where it's been.'

They looked round the room but there were no sign of any other chinchilla paw prints anywhere. 'It must have gone straight back up,' Mandy whispered, replacing the raisins. 'Shall we hide and see if it comes out again?'

'Ok,' James nodded. 'But where? We don't

want to be too close to the chimney or it might not come out at all.'

Mandy realised that James was right. She looked round. Where should they go? Her eyes suddenly fell on the rectangular serving hatch in the wall. Perfect! If they pulled the little door back they could watch from the kitchen. 'Look!' she said to James. 'Let's watch through there.'

'Great!' he agreed.

They hurried through to the kitchen and carefully pulled back the door of the hatch, trying to make as little noise as possible. It was an ideal place to watch from.

'I hope it likes its bath,' James said as they carried two chairs over to the serving hatch.

Mandy frowned. 'We can't keep calling it "it",' she said. 'We should think of a name.' She looked around the kitchen for inspiration and saw one of her parents' cassettes – *The Mikado* – lying on the table. 'We'll call it Gilbert!' she said, seeing the names Gilbert and Sullivan on the cassette box.

'But what if it's a girl,' James objected.

'I think it's a boy,' said Mandy. 'And if it's a girl then we can just change her name to Gilly.'

'OK,' James agreed. 'Well, in that case, I hope *Gilbert* likes his bath.'

'Me too,' said Mandy with a grin.

By teatime there was still no sign of Gilbert. James had to go back home and it was time for Mandy to help in evening surgery. 'I'll watch this evening,' she said as James got on to his bike. 'Come round again tomorrow.'

'OK!' he called. 'Make sure you ring me if anything exciting happens.'

'I will!' Mandy promised.

After supper, Mandy settled down to watch in earnest. She even ate her supper sitting by the serving hatch.

'So what if I want to watch some television?' Mr Hope said, coming up behind her and taking her empty plate away.

Mandy turned to him in dismay. 'Dad! You can't!' She saw the twinkle in his eyes and relaxed.

'Don't worry. I'll read a magazine instead.' He shook his head. 'But I hope this chinchilla comes out soon.'

'Me too,' said Mandy.

Mrs Hope turned some music on quietly and

sat down at the table with a book. Mr Hope joined her with his magazine, and for the next few hours the family sat in the kitchen, for once undisturbed by emergency calls.

At eleven o'clock, Emily Hope stood up. 'Time for bed,' she said, yawning. 'Come on, Mandy. You too.'

'But Mum!' Mandy had been looking through the rest of the chinchilla book as she waited for Gilbert to appear. 'Chinchillas are nocturnal. Gilbert's more likely to come out at night. I've got to stay up!'

'Gilbert!' Mr Hope chuckled. 'Where did you get that name from?'

Mandy pointed to the cassette on the table. 'I suppose it's better than Sullivan,' said Mr Hope, raising his eyebrows.

'Well, whatever he's called, you're not going to watch for him any longer tonight,' Mrs Hope said firmly to Mandy. 'Come on. Bed!'

With a sigh, Mandy gave in. Maybe Gilbert would come out tomorrow . . .

Six

As soon as Mandy woke up the next morning, one thought shot through her mind: Gilbert! Pulling on some shorts and a T-shirt, she hurried downstairs as quietly as she could. Had he come out from the chimney yet? She peeped through the serving hatch in the kitchen. Disappointment surged through her. Nothing seemed to have changed.

Cautiously pushing open the living-room door, she inspected the food bowl. Half the pellets and both the raisins had gone. She glanced at the dust-bath. On the carpet around it was a layer of white powder. The fuller's earth left in the tin was coated with black flecks of soot. So Gilbert *had* been down from the chimney in the night!

She scouted round the room, checking behind the chairs and under the sofa. But, apart from a slightly chewed bit at the bottom of one of the chair legs, there was no sign of Gilbert. It looked like he had retreated to his sooty hiding-place again.

Giving up the search, Mandy refilled the food and water bowls, replaced the fuller's earth in the dust-bath, and then hurried off to do her morning chores. She would come and keep watch for Gilbert later but first she had to feed and clean out the animals in the residential unit.

Slipping on her shoes, she went through to the surgery. A sleepy West Highland terrier got unsteadily to his feet and wagged his short, stumpy tail as she opened the door to the residential unit. 'Morning, Hamish,' Mandy said. The little dog had been in for an operation on one of his back legs. She checked his stitches. 'Are you ready for your breakfast?' she asked him.

A rabbit and a white hamster watched her from their cages opposite as she emptied Hamish's water bowl out. She heard the sound of tyres on the gravel outside and looked out of the window. Bill Ward, the Welford postman, was coming up the drive in his van. He stopped and jumped out with a pile of envelopes in his hand. Would one of them be Minnie's biopsy results from the lab? Mandy hurried out to meet him.

'Morning, Mandy!' Bill said, handing her the letters. 'How are you?'

'Fine. How are Delilah and Daisy?' she asked. Delilah and Daisy were Bill's Persian cat and kitten.

'Grand,' Bill smiled. 'You should come and see them.'

'I will,' Mandy promised.

Bill looked up at the sky. 'Looks like there might be a storm brewing,' he said, going back to his van. 'I'd better be on my way.'

As he drove off, Mandy looked up at the sky. The air was close and heavy and dark clouds were gathering on the horizon. It looked as if Bill was right.

The front door opened. 'Was that the post?' Mrs Hope said, looking out.

Mandy hurried over and handed her the letters. 'Is there anything from the lab about Minnie?' she asked hopefully.

Her mother leafed quickly through the envelopes. Reaching the end of the little pile she shook her head. 'No, sorry, love.' Her green eyes were sympathetic. 'Like I said, it normally takes a week.'

Mandy sighed. It was so difficult, waiting and not knowing. And she knew that if it was hard for her, it must be far worse for Amy.

'Any sign of Gilbert this morning?' her mother said, obviously trying to cheer her up by changing the subject.

Mandy shook her head. 'But he's been out of the chimney overnight. Some of the food's gone and he seems to have used the dust-bath. I'm going to keep watch later.'

Mrs Hope nodded. 'He should be getting a bit calmer now. You might be lucky.'

'I hope so,' said Mandy.

'What a way to spend half-term!' said James a

little while later, as they sat staring through the serving hatch. But he was grinning and Mandy knew he didn't mean it. If there was an animal in trouble he would do anything he could to help it, no matter how much patience it took.

'We couldn't be outside in this weather anyway,' she said, glancing at the kitchen window. Shortly after James had arrived, it had started to rain, and now great splashy drops were splattering against the glass.

'True!' James said, gazing back into the living-room. The next instant he grabbed her arm. 'Look!' he whispered, staring at the chimney.

Mandy followed his gaze. A little patch of soot fell from the chimney and then another and them . . .

'Gilbert!' she whispered in delight, as a very sooty chinchilla emerged from the chimney. The little creature landed in the fireplace and crouched down, his body tense. Looking round timidly, he started to creep towards the food bowl.

'Oh, poor thing!' Mandy breathed, her heart immediately going out to the frightened little animal whose heavy, beige fur was coated with fine black soot. His dark eyes flicked constantly round the room and his movements were cautious and jerky. Reaching the food bowl, he seized a sunflower seed greedily in his front paws.

'Do you think he'll have a bath?' James whispered to Mandy as Gilbert balanced on his back legs and started to nibble at the top of the sunflower seed.

Mandy held up crossed fingers. 'I hope so.'

Gilbert finished both the sunflower seeds and the raisins. After sniffing half-heartedly at the rabbit pellets, he ran over to the bread tin and looked over the edge. Mandy held her breath. *Please*, she thought. She was longing to see the little chinchilla take a dust-bath. But, just as it looked as though Gilbert was about to hop in, a low, ominous rumbling sound was heard from outside. Gilbert froze for a second and then sat up dead straight, every muscle tense.

CRASH!

'Oh no!' gasped Mandy as the clap of thunder burst over the house. With a frightened squeak, Gilbert leaped into the air and shot back up the chimney.

James and Mandy looked at each other in dismay. 'Well, that's blown it!' said James.

Mandy's heart sank further as a flash of lightning split the sky outside. There was no way Gilbert was going to come down the chimney again while the storm was raging.

'Wow! Look at the rain!' James said, getting up and going over to the window. The rain was beating down in straight lines, bouncing off the drive and the bonnet of Mr Hope's Land-rover. 'I'm glad I'm not out in that!'

A flash of forked lightning was followed by another clap of thunder.

Mandy looked at the chimney through the hatch. *Poor Gilbert*, she thought, *he must be terrified!* Going through to the living-room she kneeled down by the chimney and peered up it, but there was no sign of the chinchilla.

James came and joined her. Mandy turned to him with worried eyes. 'What are we going to do? You saw what he looked like. He was scared stiff, and that was *before* the storm started.'

James pushed a hand through his hair. 'I don't think there's much that we *can* do,' he said. 'We've just got to wait until he comes out and

starts trusting us enough to let us catch him.'

'But that could be ages!' Mandy protested, getting up and going back through to the kitchen. She sat down at the table. 'What if he gets ill? What if all the dust and soot is really bad for him?' She put her head in her hands. 'Oh, if only he knew we want to help him.'

'We're going to have to find his owner,' James said. 'Gilbert's scared of us but surely he won't be nervous with them.'

Mandy stared at him. *Gilbert's owner*! She had been so busy thinking about looking after

Gilbert and getting him down from the chimney that she had forgotten about their plans to try to find out whom he belonged to. 'Of course!' she exclaimed. 'We were going to put an advert in the paper.'

She jumped to her feet and, grabbing last week's copy of the *Walton Gazette* out of the magazine rack, quickly spread it out on the table. James was right! If anyone could get Gilbert down from the chimney quickly it would be his owner. Both her dad and the chinchilla book said that although chinchillas were wary with strangers they were normally bold and affectionate with people they knew. She opened the paper at the back page and pointed to the 'Lost and Found' section. 'We can put an advert in here,' she said. 'The paper comes out on Friday so the advert would be out in three days.' Carried away by her enthusiasm, she grabbed a pen. 'Come on, let's think of what to say.'

'Wait a sec!' James was reading a piece of information at the top. He shook his head. 'It says here that adverts for "Lost and Found" have to be in by the Friday before. That means we've missed the deadline for this week's paper. If we put an advert in then it's not going to come out until a *week* on Friday.'

'But we can't wait that long!' Mandy exclaimed. 'Gilbert can't stay up the chimney until then!'

'So, time for Plan B then,' said James.

'Plan B?' Mandy asked.

'Well . . .' A thoughtful frown creased James's forehead. 'You saw Gilbert first at the bus stop. So there's strong possibility that his owner lives near there. Why don't we go and knock on all the doors of the houses round there and see if anyone has lost him?'

'James, that's brilliant!' Mandy cried, bounding to her feet. 'You're a genius! Gilbert must have come from round there. We could find his owner today! Let's go!'

James looked out of the window as another flash of lightning shot jagged across the sky and a roll of thunder crashed loudly. 'What, now?'

Mandy paused for a moment. 'Oh, the storm will have stopped by the time we get our shoes and coats on,' she said. 'It's dying down already. Come on!' She hurried to the hall cupboard and pulled out two long, waterproof coats. 'We can wear these.'

They had just reached the door when Mrs Hope came through from the surgery. 'What on earth are you doing?' she said, looking at them dressed in the long, bright-yellow macs.

'Going to Walton,' said Mandy. 'We're going to find Gilbert's owner.'

'In *this* weather?' Mrs Hope said incredulously.

'It's only rain,' Mandy said. 'The thunderstorm's almost stopped. We've got to find his owner as quickly as possible. He might come down the chimney for them.' She saw her mother's raised eyebrows. 'We need to get him down from there as soon as possible!'

'I agree,' said Mrs Hope firmly. 'But you are certainly not going out on your bikes in this.' She stepped in front of the door. 'You can wait until the weather clears up.'

'But, Mum . . .'

'Sorry, Mandy. The answer's no.'

Mandy saw that she had no choice but to give in. Reluctantly she started to take off her coat.

Mrs Hope smiled gently at her. 'I'm sure it won't be long before the rain stops. Another hour or two is hardly going to matter, is it?'

But it wasn't just an hour or two. All day the rain pounded down relentlessly and the wind raged. It was agony having to wait. Mandy couldn't relax for a second. All she wanted to do was to find Gilbert's owner so they could help coax the chinchilla down from the chimney. She and James spent the day by the hatch, watching for Gilbert to come out.

'He might venture down again now it's stopped thundering,' James said hopefully. However, Gilbert seemed to have decided that it was safer to stay up the chimney that day. They saw no sign of him.

By four-thirty the rain had cleared just enough for James to cycle home, although Mrs Hope still made him borrow one of the bright-yellow macs.

'I feel like a banana,' he grumbled.

'You look like one!' Mandy grinned.

Pulling a face at her, he got on to his bike. 'See you tomorrow if the weather's OK!' he called as he cycled away down the drive, the mac flapping about in the wind.

As soon as Mandy woke up the next morning,

she ran over to the window. The rain had cleared and the sky was washed a pale forget-me-not blue. Throwing on some clothes, she raced downstairs to do her morning chores. The sooner they were done, the sooner she and James could go into Walton!

'You're in a hurry this morning,' Mrs Hope commented as Mandy dashed into the kitchen.

Mandy nodded. 'James and I are going to try and find Gilbert's owner,' she said. 'Is it all right if I miss morning surgery today?'

Emily Hope turned to her husband, who was reading the paper. 'What do you think?' she asked.

'Hmmm. I'm not sure about that,' Adam Hope said, a smile hovering at the corners of his mouth.

'*Dad!*' Mandy said.

He grinned. 'Of course you can go! Much as I like these quiet evenings in the kitchen I'm not sure I can go without my living-room for ever. In fact, maybe you shouldn't come back until you've *found* Gilbert's owner!' He got to his feet and propelled her towards the door. 'Go on! Go!'

'Dad! I've got to phone James first!' Mandy laughed, ducking away from him. She ran to the phone and tapped in James's number.

Mrs Hunter answered. 'James is still in bed, Mandy,' she said, sounding rather surprised at the early-morning call.

'Please can you get him?' Mandy begged. 'It's important!'

A few minutes later, a very sleepy-sounding James picked up the phone. 'Hello,' he mumbled.

'James!' Mandy cried. 'It's a really nice day! We can go to Walton!'

'Walton?' said James, sounding confused.

'Yes!' Mandy sighed in exasperation, and then explained. 'To see if we can find Gilbert's owner, of course. I'll meet you at the Fox and Goose in fifteen minutes. Don't be late!'

She rang off, shaking her head. James was useless in the mornings!

'Here,' said Mrs Hope, handing her a piece of buttered toast. 'Eat this before you go.'

Mandy took big mouthfuls, sitting on the floor and pulling on her trainers at the same time. She didn't want to waste a second's time.

Finding Gilbert's owner was vital.

Swallowing the last of the toast, she jumped to her feet. 'See you later!' she called to her mum and dad, running out of the door and not waiting for their reply.

Lost!
One beige chinchilla
missing since Friday
15th May.
Please phone if you
have seen him.

Seven

Mandy and James stopped their bikes by the
bus stop where Mandy had first seen Gilbert.
'So where do we start?' she said, looking down
the street.

James pointed to the row of terraced houses
on the same side as the bus stop. 'What about
those houses there? We could start at this end
and work our way along the street.'

'OK.' Feeling slightly nervous, Mandy went
up to the first door and knocked loudly. She
waited for a couple of minutes, but there was
no reply.

'They're probably out at work,' James said.

Mandy nodded in agreement.

James was about to knock on the door of the second house when Mandy stopped him. 'Not this one,' she said, frowning. 'This is where that old man lives. You know, the one who chased the cat out. He can't be Gilbert's owner – he obviously hates animals.'

James could see that they would be wasting their time. Missing out the old man's house, they carried on to the next house. At the fourth house they finally got their first reply. An old woman opened the door and cautiously peered round it.

'Yes?' she said, looking at them suspiciously. Mandy tried to smile reassuringly.

'We were wondering if you had lost a chinchilla or if you knew anyone nearby who had lost a chinchilla?' James said, very politely.

'A chinchilla?' said the woman, shaking her head firmly. 'No, I don't know anything about those.' Without giving them a chance to say anything more, she abruptly shut the door. Mandy's heart sank. She hoped everyone wasn't going to be so unfriendly.

'Come on, let's try the next house,' James said.

They got no reply at that house but at the one after a woman answered the door. She held a small girl by the hand. 'Hello,' she said, looking at them curiously. 'Can I help you?'

'We were wondering if you had lost a chinchilla or if you knew anyone nearby who might have?' James asked again.

Seeing the woman's puzzled expression, Mandy added quickly, 'It's like a sort of cross between a rabbit and a squirrel, round and fluffy.'

'It doesn't belong to us, I'm afraid,' said the woman, shaking her head. 'We don't have any pets.' Mandy and James said their thanks and were about to turn to go, when the little girl pulled at the woman's hand and whispered something in her ear.

'Wait a minute!' the woman said suddenly, stopping them in their tracks. 'Tamsin's just reminded me. We saw a poster about a lost pet. There was a picture on it. It was fluffy and it did look a little bit like a rabbit.'

Mandy's eyes lit up hopefully. 'Where was the poster?'

'Just down the street,' the woman said. 'On one of the lampposts.'

'Brilliant!' James said. 'Thank you so much!'

Mandy and James jumped on their bikes and raced to the bottom of the street. From a distance they spotted a lamppost that seemed to have something stuck to it. Hope filled Mandy's heart. Finding Gilbert's owner looked like it was going to be much easier than she'd expected. Reaching the lamppost she skidded to a halt and eagerly scanned the poster. It was ripped, but a badly photocopied photograph of a chinchilla could still be made out! 'It's Gilbert!' Mandy exclaimed, peering at it. 'Look, James! I'm sure it is!'

She quickly read the words:

Lost! One beige chinchilla missing since Friday 15th May. Information wanted. Please ring Mr

But there the poster ended. The name and telephone number had been torn off. Bitter disappointment flooded through Mandy.

'Maybe there are some more posters on other

lampposts,' James suggested. 'People normally put up loads. Let's try the next street.'

Realising he was right, Mandy cheered up and cycled after him towards the next street. There they found a lamppost with a scrap of white paper attached, but the rest of the poster had vanished. 'The wind must have torn it off in the storm!' Mandy said, her heart sinking.

There was no sign of any other posters anywhere. Mandy didn't think she could bear it. It was so frustrating to be so close to finding Gilbert's owner and yet to fail. 'What are we going to do?' she asked her friend, despairingly.

But James had run out of good ideas. He shrugged. 'I guess we'd better just put an advert in the paper after all.'

Mandy thought of Gilbert. He was so scared and unhappy. 'We can't wait another ten days!' she objected.

'But what else *can* we do?' said James.

Their spirits low, they started to wheel their bikes up the road. Seeing the pet shop ahead, Mandy remembered the chinchilla pellets and sepiolita. She checked in her pocket and found her purse. 'Shall we call in at the pet shop and see if the things we ordered have come in?' she said.

'Might as well,' James replied.

The doorbell tinkled as they went in. Expecting to see Geoff or Mrs Kearney, the part-time assistant, they were surprised to find a man of about fifty behind the counter. His sleeves were rolled up and he had a hearty smile. 'Good morning!' he greeted them cheerfully. 'How may I help you?'

'Um . . . we've come to collect some chinchilla pellets and sepiolita,' Mandy said. 'I ordered them by phone the other day.'

'Righty-ho!' said the man. 'I'll go and look in the back.'

'Who's that?' James whispered as the assistant disappeared.

Mandy shrugged. 'He must be new.' They had to wait quite a while. At last the man came back with one sack of pellets and another of powder.

'Sorry about the delay!' he said. 'It's only my third day here and I'm still finding my way around.' He extended his hand over the counter. 'My name's Jim,' he said. 'Are you regular customers?'

Mandy nodded and shook his hand. 'I'm Mandy.'

'And I'm James,' James said. 'We often come in here.'

Jim totted up the bill. 'And you've got a chinchilla, I see,' he said, looking at the bags on the counter.

'Well, not really,' Mandy said. She saw Jim's puzzled expression. 'We're just looking after one,' she explained. 'We found it and now we're trying to find its owner.' She had a sudden thought. 'You don't know anyone who has lost a chinchilla, do you?'

Jim shook his head. 'Sorry.'

James frowned. 'You don't know anyone else in Walton who keeps chinchillas, do you? I mean, is there anyone else who comes in here to buy chinchilla things?'

Mandy's eyes flew to his face. Of course! Gilbert's owner would have to get chinchilla supplies from somewhere. Maybe they came into the pet shop. She looked eagerly at Jim, but he was shaking his head again.

'Sorry,' he said. 'I can't help you there. You're the first people I've sold chinchilla supplies to, but like I said I've only been working here for three days. You really need to ask Geoff.'

'Will he be in later?' Mandy asked.

Jim spread his hands. 'He's off today, I'm afraid, but he'll be here tomorrow. Why don't you try calling in or ringing tomorrow morning?'

'We will,' James said, exchanging a hopeful look with Mandy. 'Thanks.'

When Mandy and James got back to Animal Ark they replaced Gilbert's rabbit pellets with the chinchilla pellets and swapped the fuller's earth in the bread tin for a layer of sepiolita. 'It looks almost the same,' said James, as he emptied in the white powder.

'Let's hope Gilbert likes it,' said Mandy, placing one raisin and two sunflower seeds next to the food bowl.

Leaving the room, they went through to the kitchen to watch.

After a bit, James nudged Mandy. 'Look!' he said, as soot began to fall from the chimney. A couple of seconds later, Gilbert came scrambling down and dropped on to the stone hearth. He looked round cautiously for a long moment and then crept over to the bowls, leaving a trail of soot behind him. He lapped at the water, but after having a quick sniff turned his nose up at the chinchilla pellets.

'He doesn't seem to like them very much,' Mandy whispered.

'That's because he likes the raisins and sunflower seeds better,' said James, watching Gilbert scamper over to the treats. The little chinchilla picked up a raisin and nibbled on it. After polishing it off, he ran over to the dust-bath and looked over the top.

Mandy gripped James's arm. 'Do you think he's going to go in?'

Before James had a chance to reply Gilbert had hopped over the side of the bread tin. With one swift movement he flipped himself over on his back and rolled ecstatically. Jumping back on to his feet, he spun round and then was down on his back again. White powder floated up into the air as he flipped and rolled and flipped and rolled. He looked like a spinning top.

Mandy grinned at James in delight. 'He loves it!' she said.

Gilbert hopped out and shook himself. Powder and soot flew off him and they could see his sandy beige colouring again. His large ears twitched. They were the same pale pink as the tip of his nose and his tiny feet, which were covered in very fine white hairs. He sat up on his hind legs. His dark eyes looked round and then, spotting the piece of apple that Mandy had put out that morning, he scampered over and started to gnaw rather thoughtfully at it, his bushy tail sticking out behind him.

He looked so sweet that Mandy smiled. 'Don't you wish you could pick him up?'

James nodded. 'I wonder if he'll ever let us.'

'He seems a bit calmer today,' said Mandy. 'What do you think he'll do if I go in?'

James looked doubtful. 'Probably run back up the chimney.'

Mandy looked at Gilbert happily nibbling on the piece of apple. If they didn't find his owner then they were going to have to start taming him themselves. 'I'm going to try,' she said. 'I'll just go in, not right up to him but just to see if he'll let me be in the same room.'

Very slowly she opened the living-room door.

Hearing the slight creak, Gilbert ran back towards the chimney. He stopped on the hearth and looked at her. Mandy hardly dared to breathe. After a bit, he seemed to decide that she was probably harmless. Keeping one wary eye on her, he hopped over to the poker and started to gnaw on the wooden handle.

Mandy crept quietly and slowly into the room. She crouched down a little way off. 'Good boy,' she murmured in a low voice. 'There's a good boy.'

Gilbert turned his head towards her. Mandy

stifled a gasp. On one side of the chinchilla's neck a patch of fur, about the size of a five-pence piece, was missing. The rough circle of bare skin was pink and sore-looking. Feeling worried, she edged closer. What was the matter with him? she wondered. Had he injured himself?

All of a sudden, Gilbert seemed to decide that she had got too close. He leaped away from the poker and with one agile bound jumped up the chimney.

Mandy sat back on the floor frowning. She didn't like the look of that patch of pink skin at all.

James, who had been watching it all through the hatch, came hurrying in. 'That was good. He let you get quite close.' He saw the frown on her face. 'What's up?'

Mandy explained about Gilbert's neck. 'I think I'd better tell Dad,' she said anxiously.

They found Mr Hope leafing through the big appointments diary in the waiting-room. 'What can I do for you?' he said, looking up with a smile as they came hurrying through.

Mandy told him what she had seen. 'Gilbert's

skin was bright pink and it looked as if his fur had fallen out.'

Mr Hope scratched his beard. 'It sounds like a fungal infection rather than an injury, although I can't be sure without examining him.'

'Is it serious?' James asked.

'We should be able to treat it,' Mr Hope said. 'What we need to do is to add some fungicide powder to his dust-bath.' He led the way through to one of the consulting rooms and took out a plastic container of white powder from the cupboard. 'Change his bath and put about a tablespoon of this in with the fresh sepiolita and' – he got out a brown bottle with a dropper in the top – 'give him a raisin with a drop of this on twice a day for the next three days.'

Mandy took the container and the bottle. 'How did he get it, do you think?' she asked.

Mr Hope knitted his eyebrows. 'It's hard to say, probably because of this warm weather, that and the stress that he's experiencing. Did you have any luck finding his owner?'

Mandy shook her head. 'But we're going to

ring Geoff at the pet shop tomorrow and ask him if anyone else comes in to buy chinchilla supplies,' she said.

'Good idea,' said Mr Hope. His blue eyes looked serious. 'The sooner we get Gilbert down from that chimney the better. If he stays up there much longer, I'm afraid his health may really start to deteriorate.'

Mandy looked at James. Poor Gilbert! If Geoff couldn't help them then *what* were they going to do?

James arrived at nine o'clock sharp the next morning. 'Here goes,' said Mandy as she picked up the phone and dialled the number of Pets' Parlour. She looked at James while the phone rang at the other end. He held up crossed fingers. They both knew that it was vitally important that they found Gilbert's owner as soon as possible

'Good morning. Pets' Parlour.' It was Geoff.

'Hi,' Mandy said quickly. 'It's Mandy Hope.' She explained what she wanted to know.

'We *do* have one customer who comes in for chinchilla supplies,' Geoff said. 'Hang on a sec.

Let me get the order book.' Mandy could hear him leafing through the pages. 'Yes,' said Geoff suddenly. 'Here it is. A Mr Sorrel. It's a Walton number: 668213. I don't know if he's lost a chinchilla, but it might be worth giving him a ring.'

'Thanks!' Mandy scribbled the number on to the piece of paper. She put the phone down.

'Well?' James asked.

Mandy showed him the number. 'Geoff says there is someone and he's called Mr Sorrel,' she said.

'But has he lost a chinchilla?' James asked.

Mandy picked up the phone. 'There's only one way to find out!'

Eight

'Hello, Sorrel speaking,' said a man's voice at the other end of the line.

'Hello.' Mandy wondered how to begin and decided to just plunge straight in. 'Umm, I know this might sound rather strange but I was wondering whether you had lost a chinchilla – a beige one?' She held her breath, waiting for the man's reply. What would he say? Was he Gilbert's owner?

'A beige chinchilla?' Mr Sorrel's heavy Yorkshire voice rose in excitement. 'Aye! Aye, I have! Have you found him?'

'Yes!' Mandy gave a delighted thumbs-up signal to James. The words tumbled out of her. 'He's at my house,' she gasped. 'My name's Mandy Hope. I live at Animal Ark – the vets in Welford.'

Mr Sorrel's voice suddenly sounded very disappointed. 'Well, I'm not sure it can be my chinchilla then, lass,' he said sadly. 'I live in Walton, you see.'

'Yes, I know,' Mandy said impatiently. 'But it *is* him. He came on the bus!'

'The bus!' Mr Sorrel echoed.

Realising how strange it must sound, Mandy quickly explained about Gilbert jumping into Jean's carrier bag. The old man soon got the gist of the story.

'It sounds like it *is* Peanut then!' he said as Mandy explained how she had seen the little chinchilla running along the street by the bus stop. 'I live just by the bus stop and he went missing last Friday, just like you said.'

'Peanut?' Mandy said.

'That's his name.' Mr Sorrel's voice trembled with excitement. 'This is such good news. You don't know how pleased I am! When can I come and collect him?'

'Any time,' Mandy said. 'Umm,' she swallowed as she realised there was still something she hadn't told Mr Sorrel. 'There's just one problem. He's up our chimney at the moment.' She explained quickly. 'He's been hiding up there for three days now. And when he does come down, he won't let us anywhere near him.'

'Oh, he'll come to me,' said Mr Sorrel confidently. 'I'll be over at lunch-time. Now, how do I find you?'

Mandy gave Mr Sorrel directions to Animal Ark and then put down the phone. She was grinning from ear to ear. 'He *is* Gilbert's owner!' she exclaimed. She corrected herself. 'Peanut's owner. That's Gilbert's real name.'

'Peanut!' said James.

'I suppose it does suit him,' Mandy said. 'His fur is the colour of peanuts.'

'So when's Mr Sorrel coming round?' James asked. 'And what does he sound like?'

'Quite old but nice!' Mandy replied. 'He's coming round at lunch-time. I wonder if

Gilbert . . .' She caught herself. '. . . If Peanut will come out of the chimney for him.' She knew that Mr Sorrel had seemed confident that Peanut would come out but then he didn't know quite how frightened the little chinchilla had been over the last few days. Mandy thought of her dad's warning about Peanut's health. She hoped Mr Sorrel was going to be right!

Mandy and James were watching the driveway eagerly from the kitchen window when, just before one o'clock, an old man wearing a lightweight green overcoat and a brown hat came walking up the drive. He looked around in a rather lost sort of way. 'That must be him!' said James, jumping to his feet.

Mandy stared out of the window. 'James!' she exclaimed. 'It's that old man who lives by the bus stop. The one who chased the cat!'

James's mouth fell open. 'Are you sure?' He looked out of the window again. 'It is!' he said, looking at her. 'You're right!'

There was a knock at the door. They looked at each other. 'What do we do?' Mandy hissed.

'There's nothing we can do,' James said. 'Just open it!'

Mandy went slowly to the door. Surely Gilbert couldn't be owned by the bad-tempered old man who had chased the cat out on to the road?

'Miss Hope?' the man said as she opened the door. Mandy nodded and the man extended his hand. 'I'm Mr Sorrel.'

'Hi,' Mandy said. 'Ummm . . . call me Mandy.' Mr Sorrel obviously didn't recognise her. She remembered her manners. 'Come in,' she said. 'This is my friend, James. He's been helping look after Gilb— Peanut.'

'Pleased to meet you,' Mr Sorrel said, offering his hand to James, who shook it awkwardly. Mr Sorrel stepped inside, wiping his feet carefully on the mat before removing his hat and coat. James took them and hung them up for him.

'Peanut's through this way,' Mandy explained. She led the way through to the living-room. 'He's up that chimney.' She looked at James, who raised his eyebrow. What would Mr Sorrel do to coax his chinchilla down? 'By the way,' Mandy continued, 'he seems very nervous and you should know that he's got a bit of a skin infection. But my dad told us how to treat it.'

Mr Sorrel nodded and then made his way cautiously towards the chimney. He kneeled down and started to make a low, soft chirping noise in the back of his throat.

For a moment nothing happened and then Mandy saw the tell-tale smattering of soot fall from the chimney. The next instant, Peanut came scrambling down. He landed in the fireplace, a sooty ball of fluff. Sitting up on his back paws, he looked at the old man.

'Here, little lad,' the old man murmured. He clucked his tongue. For a moment Peanut looked as if he couldn't believe his eyes, but then with an answering chirrup he dropped on to all fours and streaked the short distance across the carpet to where Mr Sorrel was kneeling. Peanut leaped on to the old man's knee, scampered up his jumper and came to a rest on Mr Sorrel's shoulder, his head nuzzling against the old man's ear. 'There, there.' Mr Sorrel reached up a hand and gently stroked the little chinchilla under the chin. 'You're safe now,' he soothed.

Mandy exchanged astonished glances with

James. After all their attempts to get Peanut down from the chimney she had never dreamed it would be so easy. She looked at the little chinchilla nuzzling in delight against his master's cheek. He and his owner obviously adored each other.

Mr Sorrel took Peanut off his shoulder and examined him, his fingers gently probing through the chinchilla's thick fur. 'It looks like just a simple fungal infection,' he said, reaching the missing patch. 'It should clear up in no time.'

Looking at Mr Sorrel fussing over the

chinchilla, Mandy could hardly believe that he was the same man who had chased a cat out of his house straight on to the road. The words blurted out of her before she could stop them. 'I don't understand,' she said. 'How can you like chinchillas so much and not cats?'

'Cats?' Mr Sorrel frowned at her and then realisation slowly dawned. 'You're the lass who told me off for shooing that cat out of my house,' he said in astonishment.

Mandy nodded. 'It almost got run over.' Her eyes searched his lined face. It just didn't make sense.

Mr Sorrel sighed. 'I know it was hasty of me, but I was only trying to protect the chinchillas.' He shrugged. 'Also, I'm allergic to cat hair.'

'But if you're allergic to cats why aren't you allergic to chinchillas?' James asked with a frown.

'People with fur allergies often *aren't* allergic to chinchillas,' Mr Sorrel explained. 'Which is one of the things that makes them such good pets.'

But Mandy had something else on her mind. What had Mr Sorrel just said? 'Chinchillas,' she repeated. 'You've got *more* than one?'

'I've got two,' Mr Sorrel said, nodding. 'I bought my second one, Woodstock, six months ago. He's a quality chinchilla. I take him to shows.'

Mandy smiled. Woodstock and Peanut! They were great names. 'Are they friends?' she asked.

'Not at all.' Mr Sorrel's face crinkled up with concern. 'In fact, just the opposite.' He stroked Peanut's head. 'I've got a real problem. This little lad hates me giving Woodstock any attention. He's always been affectionate and doesn't seem to like sharing me at all. Whenever I take Woodstock out of his cage to try and groom him or hold him, Peanut tries to escape.'

'Is that what happened the other day?' Mandy asked curiously.

Mr Sorrel nodded. 'I'd taken Woodstock out to give him a good grooming and Peanut must have been feeling jealous because he escaped from his cage. About the same moment I realised he'd got out, I also saw the cat getting in through my kitchen window. I panicked and chased it out of the door. Peanut must have run out while the door was open.'

Mandy felt she was beginning to understand Mr Sorrel's behaviour that day at the bus stop. He had only chased the cat because he had been worried about Peanut being loose in the house. 'How did he get out of his cage?' she asked.

'He's worked out a way of opening the door,' Mr Sorrel explained. 'He gets hold of the back part of the door catch in his mouth and then kicks back with his feet until the door opens.' He stroked Peanut's head. 'He lets himself out whenever he thinks he is being ignored. Normally it doesn't matter because I've made the house safe for him to be out and I keep all the windows shut. But last Friday it was so muggy I just had to open a window and of course then that cat got in.'

Mandy shivered as she thought what could have happened to Peanut. She looked at him cuddling into Mr Sorrel's jumper. 'Will he let me touch him?' she asked.

Mr Sorrel nodded. 'Just hold out your hand so he can sniff you first,' he said.

Mandy slowly put her hand out – she didn't

want to alarm Peanut in any way. The chinchilla sniffed her fingers. Very slowly she started to tickle under his chin. He closed his eyes and rubbed the side of his head against her fingers. She smiled. He was so sweet! She was really going to miss taking care of him. But she was *very* glad he was out of the chimney.

'What are you going to do about Peanut being jealous of Woodstock?' she asked softly.

'I don't know,' Mr Sorrel admitted, his eyes worried. 'I've got a show on Saturday and I need to spend some time tomorrow getting Woodstock ready. If I know Peanut, he'll try and escape again.'

'Can't you fix the door so he can't open it?' James asked.

Mr Sorrel nodded. 'I guess I'll have to. But he'll be so miserable then. Still I can't give him attention and groom Woodstock at the same time, can I?' He suddenly looked at them as if he'd had an idea. 'I don't suppose you would like to come over and play with him, would you?' he said. 'It would only be for a bit, just while I groom Woodstock.' He quickly shook his head and looked away. 'No, no,' he said gruffly. 'I shouldn't have asked. I'm sure you've got plenty of other things you'd rather be doing.'

'We haven't!' Mandy exclaimed. 'We'd love to help!'

'Definitely!' said James.

Mr Sorrel looked at them as if he didn't quite believe what he was hearing. 'Are you sure?' he asked.

'Positive!' Mandy said. 'I'll really miss having Peanut here. It would be brilliant to come and spend some time with him.'

'Oh . . . well, right then.' Mr Sorrel looked very pleased. 'Well, in that case should we say about half past ten?'

Mandy grinned. 'We'll be there!' Her eyes shone. She would get to cuddle and play with Peanut *and* see another chinchilla. What could be better than that?

When Mandy and James stopped their bikes outside Mr Sorrel's house the next day, they saw Amy Fenton coming out of the pet shop with a bag of bedding in her hand. 'Amy!' Mandy called, waving.

Amy came over. 'Hi!'

'How's Minnie?' James asked, looking at her in concern.

'OK, thanks,' Amy replied. 'The stitches don't seem to be bothering her at all.' Now she was closer to them, Mandy could see how strained she was looking. There were dark shadows under her eyes. 'I was just getting some more bedding for her,' she said, holding up the bag. She managed a faint smile. 'They had some really sweet baby mice in there.'

'I know, I saw them last Friday,' Mandy said.

Amy blinked. 'They reminded me of how Minnie was when she was young.' Tears sprang to her eyes. 'Sorry,' she muttered, brushing her sleeve quickly across her face and turning to go.

Mandy stopped her. 'It's all right,' she said, her eyes bright with sympathy. 'We understand.'

Amy nodded and then, swallowing hard, turned and hurried on her way.

'Poor Amy,' James said quietly as they watched her go.

Mandy sniffed back the tears. 'Oh, why do animals have to get old?' she exclaimed.

'Come on,' James said, changing the subject.

'Mr Sorrel will be waiting.'

They knocked on Mr Sorrel's door. He opened it quickly. 'Hello there,' he said, a smile creasing up his face. 'Come in. You can leave your bikes in here.'

Mandy and James squeezed their bikes into the narrow red-tiled hallway. The house had an old-fashioned feel and the air smelled slightly of boiled cabbage.

'This way,' Mr Sorrel said, indicating a room to the left. 'I keep Peanut and Woodstock in here.'

Mandy and James followed him into a small sitting-room with a threadbare green carpet, a gas fire and an old faded three-piece suite. 'Wow!' Mandy exclaimed suddenly.

Two enormous wire chinchilla cages stood on two low tables against one of the walls. Each cage was almost a metre high and a metre wide and had a thick bed of pine shavings, some entwined wooden branches for the chinchillas to climb, a wheel, and a block of wood for gnawing on.

'I like to give them plenty of room to play,' Mr Sorrel said, pleased with her reaction.

Mandy and James crouched down. Peanut was in the left-hand cage, sitting on a branch. In the right-hand cage, a pure white chinchilla with grey ears and a grey nose was gnawing on a wooden block. 'That's Woodstock,' said Mr Sorrel, following their gaze.

'He's beautiful,' Mandy said, admiring the white chinchilla's luxuriant snowy-white fur and charcoal-grey ears.

'He's a bit nervous.' Mr Sorrel poked his finger through the bars of the cage. 'Woodstock,' he called, and he made the same chirping noise in the back of his throat that he had made the day before. Woodstock looked up warily. 'Come on, lad.' Looking cautiously at Mandy and James, Woodstock scampered over to the bars but then darted away again quickly. There was an angry chattering sound from the cage next door.

'Oh, poor Peanut!' Mandy said, turning to him. 'Are you jealous?'

The beige chinchilla was standing up on his back legs and chattering angrily through the bars of his cage at them. 'You see the problem,' Mr Sorrel said. He shook his head and then went over to Peanut's cage and opened the door. 'What are we going to do with you, lad?' he said, putting out both his hands.

Peanut hopped out on to his outstretched palms and looked up at Mandy and James, his eyes bright and his whiskers twitching.

Mandy couldn't help but laugh. He looked so pleased with himself now that he had finally got his master's attention.

'He's much less sooty than he was yesterday,' James commented.

'Aye. He had a good bath yesterday – with the fungicide powder in, of course,' Mr Sorrel said. 'He could do with a brush later.'

Mandy noticed two dust-baths sitting outside the cages. 'Why aren't their baths in the cages?' she asked curiously.

'They'd be in them all the time.' Mr Sorrel chuckled, stroking Peanut under the chin. 'And if they bathe too much, then their skin can start to dry out.' Cupping his hands round Peanut he brought him up close to his face. 'Now, are you going to be a good lad and play with these nice young people while I groom Woodstock?' he said.

Peanut cocked his head on one side and seemed to consider the question. *I might*, he seemed to say.

'It's probably best if we let him get to know you gradually,' Mr Sorrel said. Putting Peanut back in his cage he instructed them what to do. 'Put your hands in the cage one at a time. He'll probably sniff and may even nibble you at first, but he'll soon get used to you and let you handle him. He's a friendly little soul really.'

'Does he have a run or something to come out in?' James asked, looking round the room.

'He can come out anywhere in this room,' Mr Sorrel said as he got Woodstock out of his cage. 'It's all safe in here. There's some toys in that box there.' He pointed to a metal tin.

'Should we use treats?' Mandy asked.

'Not to get him out of his cage. If he smells raisins on your hands he might be tempted to bite you,' Mr Sorrel replied. 'But once he's out and used to you, you can come through and get some from the kitchen if you want.'

Taking Woodstock through to the kitchen to groom him, he left Mandy and James alone with Peanut.

Mandy opened the cage door. 'Who's going first?' she asked.

'You,' James said.

Peanut sat in the back of his cage and watched as Mandy slowly put a hand in. After a moment's thought he scampered over. Mandy held her breath as he sniffed at her hand; his long whiskers tickled and she had to bite her lip to stop herself from giggling. Then Peanut ran to the back of the cage and watched her warily for a moment before he came forward again. This time he crouched down and started to nibble gently on her fingers. Mandy forced herself not to move. She knew from reading the chinchilla book that chinchillas nibbled each other in greeting, but even so it was hard to keep still! She had seen pictures of a chinchilla's long front incisors and knew that it would hurt if he did decide to bite hard. But Peanut didn't bite. Instead he hopped on to her palm and sat and looked at her, his eyes bright. His little body felt surprisingly solid.

After a few moments, he hopped off again. Mandy cupped both her hands outside the cage door. Peanut scampered over and jumped out straight into them. Moving very slowly so as not to alarm him, Mandy brought the little chinchilla up to her chest and cuddled him.

Although his fur was still a little bit sooty it felt wonderfully soft and thick. She tickled under his ears and chin as she had seen Mr Sorrel do. Peanut chirped contentedly.

'Isn't he sweet?' Mandy breathed. 'I can't believe I'm actually holding him, after all this time.' James edged over and cautiously stroked the little chinchilla. Peanut didn't seem to mind at all. In his own surroundings he seemed much more confident.

'His skin is looking a bit better,' James said, gently looking at the missing patch of fur. 'It's much less pink.'

'Shall we see what he does when I put him down?' Mandy said.

James nodded, and so she gently put Peanut down on the carpet. He scampered off happily. James investigated the metal box and took out a couple of wooden tunnels and a square block with holes in. He put them on the floor. 'Here, Peanut!' But Peanut was too interested in exploring the room to come over.

'I'll go and get some treats,' Mandy said. She hurried through to the kitchen. It was at the end of the hallway. Mr Sorrel was sitting in a chair grooming Woodstock on a towel on his knee.

'Can I have some treats, please?' Mandy asked.

Mr Sorrel pointed to a tin on the table. 'There are sunflower seeds and raisins in there,' he said.

Mandy picked up the tin and looked curiously at the grooming process. Mr Sorrel was holding Woodstock gently by the tail and combing from the tip, down towards his neck, with a metal comb. Balls of white fluff were collecting on the towel.

'How often do you have to groom them?' Mandy asked, watching closely.

'Every couple of days,' Mr Sorrel said. 'It keeps the hair smooth and stops it coming out all over the cage. There's another comb and a towel over there on the roof of that cage in the corner,' he pointed out. 'You can groom Peanut if you like.'

'Yes, please!' Mandy picked up the comb and

towel from the top of the big, empty chinchilla cage in the corner.

'Are you going to get another chinchilla?' she asked, looking at the cage with interest.

Mr Sorrel nodded. 'That's going to be for my first litter of babies. I'm going to get a female.'

'You're going to breed them!' Mandy breathed. She couldn't imagine anything more wonderful than a litter of baby chinchillas. They would be adorable!

Mr Sorrel worked the comb methodically through Woodstock's hair. 'Aye. In a bit, when this lad's older. I can't really compete with the big breeders when it comes to breeding show chinchillas but I'd like to breed pets for people.'

Mandy hurried back to the sitting-room to tell James the news. She slowed as she got near to the door, not wanting to alarm Peanut by bounding in. But she needn't have worried – Peanut was all confidence in his home. He scampered over and started investigating the laces in her trainers as she told James about Mr Sorrel's plans.

For the next half hour they played with Peanut, encouraging him through the tunnels using sunflower seeds and also discovering that he was rather good at undoing shoelaces. When he was a little less energetic, they spent some time grooming him and then they put him back in his cage.

'You've been a great help,' Mr Sorrel said, bringing the beautifully groomed Woodstock through and smiling at Peanut, who was gnawing contentedly on his wood block. 'Thank you very much.'

Mandy looked admiringly at the sleek white chinchilla. 'He looks very smart. Do you think he will do well at the show?'

Mr Sorrel said. 'Well, he has won a few first prizes in the past.' He smiled. But we'll just have to wait and see this time.'

'How do the judges decide which chinchilla is best?' James asked curiously.

'It's partly conformation – that's the bone structure – and partly coat quality and colour.'

'And will there be all different colours of chinchilla there?' Mandy asked.

Mr Sorrel nodded. 'Yes, there are classes for standard greys and then classes for whites and beiges and blacks.'

'Wow!' said Mandy, her eyes lighting up at the thought of so many chinchillas all together at once.

'You . . . er . . . wouldn't like to come, would you?' Mr Sorrel asked, seeing their faces.

'We'd love to!' Mandy said.

James nodded enthusiastically. 'We'd have to ask our parents but I'm sure they'd say yes. Where is it?'

'In York,' Mr Sorrel said, showing them to the door. 'I'll be leaving about eight-thirty tomorrow morning if you can make it by then.'

'You bet!' said Mandy, as she and James wheeled their bikes towards the front door.

A chinchilla show! She wasn't going to miss that for anything!

Nine

'Bye, Mum. Bye, Dad.' Mandy gave them each a quick kiss before grabbing her purse from the table and hurrying to the door.

'Have a good day!' Mrs Hope called, putting the breakfast dishes away.

'And don't come back with any chinchillas!' Mr Hope added.

Mandy turned and shot him a quick grin. 'Not even a little tiny baby one?' she teased.

'No!' Mr Hope said firmly.

Mandy opened the front door. Bill Ward was getting out of his van with a pile of letters in his hand. 'Hello!' he said, looking at her happy face. 'You look cheerful.'

'That's because I'm off to a chinchilla show,' she said, taking the letters from him.

Bill raised his eyebrows. 'Chinchillas? What will it be next?' He headed back towards his van. 'Well, have a good time.'

'I will!' Mandy waved him off and then hurried through with the envelopes to the kitchen. 'Here!' she said, putting them down on the kitchen table and grinning at her mum and dad. 'Now I really *am* going!'

'Bye!' Mrs Hope said, picking up the post.

Mandy fetched her bike. Would James be on time or would he be late? Knowing how often he overslept, she had arranged to meet him with plenty of time to spare.

Just as Mandy was setting off, the front door opened. 'Mandy!' Mrs Hope called, running out. 'Wait!' She hurried across the gravel, a letter in her hand. 'It's Minnie's test results!'

Mandy skidded to a stop, her heart leaping into her mouth. Minnie's test results! What would they say?

'It's all right,' Mrs Hope said reassuringly,

seeing her worried face. 'It's good news! The lump was benign.' Her eyes shone.

'Mum!' Mandy shrieked, dropping her bike and racing over to fling her arms round her mother's neck. 'That's wonderful!'

'Isn't it?' Emily Hope said, hugging her back. 'Amy's going to be so pleased. Will you and James have time to call in and tell her or do you want me to ring her later?'

Excitement and delight bubbled through Mandy. 'Can we tell her?' she cried. 'We have to go past her house anyway.'

Mrs Hope nodded. 'But make sure you're not late for Mr Sorrel.'

'We won't be!' Mandy leaped on her bike, hardly able to contain her excitement. 'Bye!' she called as she cycled madly away. She couldn't wait to meet James and tell him the news.

James was waiting for her at the crossroads. His hair was tousled. 'Mum made me get up at seven o'clock!' he grumbled as she screeched to a stop beside him. 'I said I'd be early. I—'

Mandy didn't give him a chance to finish. The good news spilled out of her. 'James! Minnie's test results are back! She's OK!'

James's face split into a massive grin. 'Oh, wow! That's brilliant!'

Mandy nodded in delight. 'Mum said we can tell Amy.'

James leaped on to his bike, suddenly full of energy. 'Come on, then, what are we waiting for? Let's go!'

Amy lived in a house on Welford High Street. Dropping their bikes by the gate, Mandy and James raced up the garden path and banged on the front door. Mr Fenton, Amy's father, answered. 'Morning,' he said, looking at them in some surprise. 'What can I do for you?'

'Is Amy here please?' Mandy blurted out excitedly. 'We've got something to tell her.'

Just then Amy came hurrying to the door, looking surprised. 'I thought I heard your voice, Mandy.'

'Amy!' Mandy exploded, unable to control herself. 'Minnie's all right! The tumour was benign!'

Amy gasped. For a moment her face paled, then the colour rushed back into her cheeks. 'Really?' she gasped, looking as if she hardly dared to believe them. 'It's really true?'

'Yes!' Mandy and James said in unison, jumping around her in excitement.

'Oh!' Amy burst into tears. 'I'm not sad!' she cried, smiling at their suddenly bemused faces. 'I'm happy! I'm so, *so* happy!' She wiped her eyes as Mandy hugged her. 'It's the best news I could ever have!'

'Can we see Minnie?' James asked eagerly.

'Yes. She's upstairs. Come on!'

Mandy glanced at her watch as they raced up the stairs after Amy. It was still early. As long as they were quick they should be in plenty of time for Mr Sorrel.

'Sorry about the mess,' Amy apologised, opening her bedroom door.

But Mandy and James didn't notice the mess. Their eyes went straight to the wire cage standing on a table in the corner. There, in the centre, was Minnie. She was gnawing happily on an old cardboard tube.

Amy crouched down beside the table. 'Oh, Minnie!' she said to the little mouse.

Minnie scampered over to the bars of the cage and looked at her. *What's all this fuss about?* she seemed to say.

Amy opened the cage door and took her out. 'I love you!' she whispered, kissing the little mouse on the nose. She turned to Mandy and James, her eyes shining with happy tears. 'I know she's old and she's not going to be here for ever,' she said. 'But I couldn't bear to lose her just yet.' She let Minnie run from one hand to the other. 'It's my birthday next week and Mum and Dad have said I can get another mouse. I'm going to the pet shop to choose one this afternoon. I think it will be nice for Minnie to have a friend.'

'I hope she won't be jealous,' James said, thinking of Peanut and Woodstock.

Amy shook her head. 'Mice like company.' She kissed Minnie on the nose again. 'Aren't I lucky?' she exclaimed joyfully. 'I'm going to have two mice to love!'

Mandy and James couldn't stay long at Amy's because they knew Mr Sorrel would be waiting for them. After cycling along the Walton Road as quickly as they could, they arrived at Mr Sorrel's house just as he was coming out of the front door. He was carrying a small travelling cage covered in a piece of material, which he took over to his rather battered-looking, old grey car.

'I was beginning to wonder whether you were coming or not,' he said as they rode up to him.

'Sorry. We had something we had to do first,' Mandy said, grinning happily at James. She felt like she was walking on air. It had been so wonderful to see Amy looking happy again.

Mr Sorrel carefully put the cage on to the floor of the front passenger seat.

'Is Woodstock in there?' James asked.

Mr Sorrel nodded. 'He likes to travel in the front. I lift a piece of his cloth so he can see me and it stops him getting nervous on the journey.' He quietly shut the car door. 'Now, let's get these bikes of yours inside.'

'Is Peanut coming to the show?' Mandy asked, as they wheeled their bikes into the house.

'No. Only chinchillas that are entered are allowed to go to the shows,' Mr Sorrel replied. 'And Peanut's coat isn't of a high enough quality to compete.' He headed into the kitchen. 'I'll just get my things then we'd best be off.'

Mandy and James went through to the sitting-room. Peanut was sitting miserably at the back of his cage. His ears drooped. He seemed to know that he was going to be left behind. 'Poor thing,' Mandy said. She frowned and turned to James. 'I don't really see what the difference is between his coat and Woodstock's.'

Mr Sorrel came in behind them and overheard. 'To the novice eye there isn't much difference at all,' he told her. 'But the experts wouldn't give him a chance in a show class. It's a pity,' he sighed, shaking his head. 'He's such a friendly little lad. I would have liked to have bred from him if his coat had been better. I'm sure his babies would have made grand pets *and* he'd have liked the company of a mate.'

'But wouldn't he be jealous of a female, like he is with Woodstock?' Mandy asked.

'Providing you introduce them gradually, male and female chinchillas normally get on,' Mr Sorrel explained. 'It might have been the ideal solution. It's just a shame that his coat isn't up to scratch.'

'But couldn't you breed from him anyway?' James said. 'After all, if his babies were just going to be pets then it wouldn't really matter to owners what their coats were like.'

'James is right,' Mandy said quickly. 'Animals like dogs and cats don't have to be pedigrees to make great pets. Pet owners just want an animal that is friendly.'

Mr Sorrel scratched his head. 'I don't know. You should always really breed the best quality animals you can.'

'But why?' Mandy objected. 'I mean it's not like he has anything else wrong with him.'

'Well . . .' Mr Sorrel suddenly caught sight of the clock on the mantelpiece. 'You know, we really should be off,' he said in alarm. 'I don't want to miss Woodstock's registration!'

With one last look at poor, miserable Peanut, Mandy and James followed Mr Sorrel out to the car.

Mandy thought the chinchilla show was amazing! She had never seen anything like it in her life. There were hundreds of chinchillas lined up in wire cages on benches. Officials in white coats were bustling around, picking cages up and taking them over to a long judging table lit by bright spotlights. Owners and their helpers were filling in registration forms and grooming the chinchillas. Other people wandered along the benches looking at the chinchillas already in their cages. There was so much to see, and yet Mandy's mind couldn't help wandering back to poor little Peanut, in his cage, all alone at home. *If only there was something we could do to make him happier*, she kept thinking. *But what?*

Mr Sorrel looked round. 'First I have to register Woodstock,' he told them. He stopped one of the people in white coats and was directed to a table, where he was given a registration from and allocated a show cage with a tag to fill in and attach to it.

'They want to know his age, sex, and breeding,' Mr Sorrel said, completing the details on the form while Mandy held Woodstock's travelling cage. He handed the form in at the desk and turned to Mandy and James. 'Now let's go and find Woodstock's place.'

The show cage was situated on a long bench, surrounded on both sides by cages filled with other white chinchillas.

'Number 135,' James said, reading the black-

and-white number that had been attached to one side of the cage.

Mr Sorrel attached the pen tag to the other side. 'You have to fold down the bit with your name on,' he explained.

'So that the judging is fair?' Mandy asked.

Mr Sorrel nodded and put Woodstock's travelling box down on the bench. 'Now he needs a good brush and then we have to leave him in his show cage,' he said. It took Mr Sorrel quite a long time to give Woodstock a thorough enough grooming. Mandy looked round. There were chinchillas of all colours: black ones, white ones, beige ones and lots of different shades of grey.

'What happens now?' James asked as Mr Sorrel secured Woodstock in his cage.

'Now one of the stewards will come and take him over to that bench there and judge his colour phase.' Mr Sorrel saw their puzzled faces. 'Each colour is split into groups according to how light or dark they are. There are three phases – light, medium and dark.'

James looked round at all the white chinchillas. 'But how can a white chinchilla be light, medium or dark?'

'Whites are judged on the amount of grey hair that they have,' Mr Sorrel explained. 'They nearly all have a bit.'

Soon a man came to collect Woodstock and took him, in his cage, to the grading table, where he was compared with several other chinchillas already sitting there. 'They're not entered in the show,' Mr Sorrel informed them. 'They're just to help the stewards decide which colour phase an animal should go in.'

Mandy felt her head starting to buzz with all the information. 'When does the judging start?'

'When all the animals have been graded,' Mr Sorrel replied.

While Mandy and James waited for the judging to begin they went to get ice creams from a snack bar by the hall entrance. Mr Sorrel had warned them not to take any food or drink near the chinchillas in case they spilled anything on to an animal's coat, so they watched from a distance as the chinchillas were all graded.

'I think the judging's about to start!' Mandy said eventually, as a group of people wearing smart red-and-blue rosettes and carrying clipboards marched over towards an empty table. One by one the chinchilla cages were carried over by the stewards for judging. The white chinchillas were judged first.

Mandy and James watched as the judges examined the chinchillas' fur, checked their conformation and made copious notes. 'I hope Woodstock wins something,' James said.

They saw Woodstock being carried over to the judges' table and so they hurriedly finished their ice creams and went back to join Mr Sorrel. He was talking to a fellow exhibitor. 'Your lad's looking well, George,' he remarked.

'Aye,' the other man, George, agreed. 'But so's Woodstock.'

'Fingers crossed, eh?' said Mr Sorrel to him, with a smile. 'Maybe we'll both go home with another rosette to add to our collections.'

George scratched his balding head. He was a tall man with a weather-beaten face. Next to his large frame, Mr Sorrel looked tiny. 'You're not looking for a mate for Woodstock, are you?' George asked.

Mr Sorrel shook his head. 'Not yet. I'm going

to let him mature for a bit longer. Why, have you got something?'

George stuck his hands in the pockets of his tweed trousers and nodded. 'Aye. Pretty little thing. A standard with a good coat – light grey, she is. Very friendly.'

Mandy saw Mr Sorrel pause for a moment. 'Friendly, you say?' he said thoughtfully. George nodded. He looked as if he was about to say more when the officials returned with the two men's chinchillas.

'Well, little lad,' said Mr Sorrel, immediately giving his attention to Woodstock. 'Did you impress them, then?' He poked his fingers through the bars of the cage and encouraged the wary chinchilla forward for a tickle on the nose.

'Do you think he's likely to win something?' James asked.

'All chinchillas rated excellent are given a first-prize rosette,' Mr Sorrel said. 'I'm holding out for one of those.' He raised his eyebrows. 'He's won two before. So you never know.'

At long last, all the white chinchillas had been judged.

'Do we find out the results now?' Mandy asked. 'Or do we have to wait until all the other colours have been judged?'

'We find out now,' said Mr Sorrel, nervously knotting his hands. 'Before they go on to judge the other colour sections.'

One of the judges stepped forward. 'Here are the results of the white section. The first prize winners in class one, light phase, are . . .'

'This is Woodstock's class and phase, isn't it?' James whispered to Mandy.

She nodded eagerly.

'Number 115, Mrs Stewart; number 129, Mr Dunne . . .'

'Well done, George!' Mr Sorrel called to his friend.

'Number 135, Mr Sorrel . . .'

'Yes!' Mandy gasped in delight. Woodstock had won a first-prize rosette! She grabbed James. 'He's won!' They swung round to find Mr Sorrel smiling broadly.

'Another first!' George came over and banged him on the back. 'Congratulations!'

'You too!' said Mr Sorrel.

The judge read out the remaining three

names on his list and then paused to announce the chinchilla that had been chosen as the best in the phase. Neither Woodstock nor George's chinchilla were picked but Mr Sorrel and George weren't disappointed. 'We can't really hope to compete with the big breeders,' Mr Sorrel said, fixing his red rosette to the side of Woodstock's cage. 'They've got hundreds of animals to choose from. No. Getting a first prize is enough for me.'

Once they had all congratulated Woodstock, Mandy, James and Mr Sorrel settled down to watch some more of the judging. George came over with his chinchilla in its travelling cage. 'I'm off home now,' he said to Mr Sorrel. 'You think about that little doe of mine. She'd breed a nice litter, I'm sure.' He winked at Mandy and James.

Mr Sorrel scratched his nose. 'I'll think about it,' he said. 'You say she's friendly.'

'Bold as brass.' George replied. 'See you then.' He nodded to Mandy and James. 'Nice meeting you.'

'You too,' they chorused.

Picking up his bags, George left.

After watching the judging for a bit longer, Mandy turned to Mr Sorrel. 'What time are we staying till?' She was loving seeing all the chinchillas but she couldn't help thinking of poor Peanut all alone in his cage.

Her question seemed to pull Mr Sorrel out of deep thought. He blinked. 'Umm. I think we may go pretty soon if that's all right with you,' he said. He nodded as if he had suddenly made up his mind about something. 'There's something I want to do on the way home.'

They were driving along the main road out of York when Mr Sorrel suddenly indicated left. He turned down a street edged on both sides by red-brick terraced houses. 'You don't mind if we stop here for a minute, do you?' he asked as he parked the car halfway down the street.

Mandy and James shook their heads and watched curiously as he got out of the car and knocked at one of the houses. The front door opened.

'That's George!' Mandy said in surprise, immediately recognising the large figure in the pale blue shirt and tweed trousers.

The two men had a brief conversation and then disappeared inside the house. When Mr Sorrel appeared again, he was carrying a travelling cage hidden by a cover.

'He's bought the female!' James exclaimed as they both stared out of the window. 'The one that George told him about! He's bought a mate for Woodstock!'

Mandy felt a thrill run through her but she couldn't help feeling rather surprised. 'He said he didn't think Woodstock was ready to mate with yet.'

'He must have changed his mind,' said James.

Mr Sorrel opened the back door of the car. 'Would you mind holding on to this cage for me?' he asked, handing it in.

Mandy and James took it eagerly and settled it between them. Mandy peeped underneath the cover as Mr Sorrel got into the car. 'She's beautiful!' she breathed, looking at the silver-grey chinchilla in the cage. The little chinchilla scampered over to the bars of the cage and sat up on her back legs as if to get a closer look at Mandy's face. Mandy smiled.

'So you *are* going to breed from Woodstock,'

James said as Mr Sorrel started the car again.

'No,' Mr Sorrel said.

Mandy and James looked at him in surprise. Mr Sorrel saw their faces in his car mirror and a smile twitched at the corners of his mouth. 'That little girl's not for Woodstock. She's for Peanut,' he said.

'Peanut!' Mandy echoed. 'But you said you weren't going to breed from him.'

'I know, but you two made me change my mind.' Mr Sorrel indicated and pulled out. 'You're right. What do pet chinchilla owners care about the quality of a coat? They just want an animal that's going to be healthy, friendly and affectionate. Peanut's like that and so, by all accounts, is Lucy.'

'Lucy?' said James. 'Is that her name?'

Mr Sorrel nodded. 'That's what I'm going to call her. She and Peanut should have some fine bold babies.'

Mandy's face split into a broad grin. 'And Peanut won't have to be lonely and jealous any more!'

'Providing he takes to her,' Mr Sorrel said. 'There's no guarantee of that, of course.'

* * *

When they got back to Mr Sorrel's house they carried the two travelling cages carefully through to the kitchen and then took the large empty cage from the kitchen through to the sitting-room. Peanut was huddled in the back corner of his cage.

'Peanut!' Mandy called softly. The little chinchilla pricked up his ears and looked at her.

James helped Mr Sorrel shuffle the cages round. Lucy was to be next to Peanut on the table. 'I'll have to keep them in separate cages for at least a week,' Mr Sorrel explained. 'They'll need time to get used to each other.'

'So, how will you know if Peanut is going to like her or not?' James asked as Mr Sorrel spread a thick layer of wood shavings on the bottom of Lucy's new cage.

Mr Sorrel chuckled. 'I think we might get a fair idea. Peanut's never shy about letting me know how he feels.'

At last the cage was ready, a water bottle had been filled and a food bowl set out. 'Now the fun begins,' Mr Sorrel said, carrying Lucy's travelling cage through. Mandy crossed her fingers. Could Lucy be the perfect solution to all Peanut's problems?

After letting Lucy get used to his hand, Mr Sorrel carefully lifted her out and placed her in the cage next to Peanut. The male chinchilla took one look at her, let out a horrified chirp and raced to the back of his cage.

Mandy's heart sank.

'Oh,' James said, sounding very disappointed. 'He doesn't seem to like her very much.'

'Let's just watch,' Mr Sorrel suggested softly.

Lucy went up to the bars of her cage and, sitting up on her back paws, sniffed cautiously. Peanut watched her with wide eyes. Then Lucy crouched down on all fours and looked at him, her whiskers twitching, her black eyes sparkling. Mandy didn't think she'd ever seen such a pretty little chinchilla.

Peanut uttered a rather less horrified sounding chirp and started moving cautiously towards her. He chirped again. Then, reaching the bars of his cage, he snuffled with his whiskers and their noses met.

Mandy held her breath as the two chinchillas sniffed each other and then both jumped away and sat back on their back legs. A few seconds passed and then they approached each other again. This time they sniffed noses for longer. Lucy jumped back and squeaked. Peanut sat up on his back legs and looked round at his audience.

'So what do you think of her, lad?' Mr Sorrel said. 'Do you like her?'

Peanut bobbed his head up and down and chirped cheekily before bouncing over to the bars to see Lucy again.

Mandy grinned. 'Somehow, I think that's a yes,' she said.

Just over four months later, Mandy and James stood in Mr Sorrel's sitting-room, looking into Lucy's cage. Lucy was snoozing in a corner and two baby chinchillas, one grey and one beige, were cuddled beside her. They were just two days old.

'So what do you think of Lucy's two baby boys?' Mr Sorrel said proudly.

'They're sweet,' James said.

'Perfect!' Mandy breathed. She had been expecting the baby chinchillas to be like baby rats and mice – born hairless and blind – but

Lucy's babies were covered in fur and their dark eyes were open and bright. *They look just like miniature versions of Peanut and Lucy,* she thought, *each small enough to fit in the palm of a hand.* 'Have you got names for them yet?' she asked Mr Sorrel.

He smiled. 'Well, naming them will really be up to their new owners but just for now I've called the grey one Charlie and the beige one Linus.' He undid the cage. 'Do you want to hold them? Lucy won't mind.' Mandy and James nodded eagerly and held out their hands to take the precious bundles of fluff. Mr Sorrel passed them carefully over, the beige one to Mandy, the grey one to James.

Mandy cupped her hands gently round the tiny baby, stroking his velvet-soft fur with the tips of her fingers. He looked up at her, his long whiskers twitching, his eyes button-bright. He reminded her so much of Peanut!

In the cage next door, Peanut walked up and down, stopping occasionally to peer in at Lucy. 'How long will he have to stay in a separate cage for?' James asked, cuddling Charlie, the grey baby chinchilla. 'It won't be for long will it?'

'Just another day or so,' Mr Sorrel said. 'Male chinchillas make good fathers, but unless you want the female to get pregnant straight away again you have to keep them separated for a bit.' He bent down and made a chirruping noise to attract Peanut's attention. 'I think he's missing Lucy,' he said, tickling Peanut's nose. 'He's been off his food.'

Lucy scampered over to the bars of her cage. Peanut immediately left Mr Sorrel and ran over to meet her.

'He really does like her, doesn't he?' James said as the two chinchillas sniffed noses.

'Aye. When chinchillas mate, they mate for life,' Mr Sorrel said softly. 'There's no separating them now.'

Mandy grinned happily at James as she cuddled the warm baby chinchilla. With Lucy as his mate, Peanut need never be lonely again.

Everything had worked out perfectly for the little chinchilla after all!

Another Hodder Children's book

PUPPY IN A PUDDLE
Animal Ark 43

Lucy Daniels

Mandy Hope loves animals more than anything else. She knows quite a lot about them too: both her parents are vets and Mandy helps out in their surgery, Animal Ark.

When Mandy's dad diagnoses an under-size Old English Sheepdog puppy as deaf, Mandy feels sad for it. But it isn't until she finds another Sheepdog pup abandoned and in a sorry state, that she and James begin to be suspicious. Could a local breeder be to blame for the condition of these puppies?

ANIMAL ARK *by Lucy Daniels*

All Hodder Children's books are available at your local bookshop, or can be ordered direct from the publisher. Just tick the titles you would like and complete the details below. Prices and availability are subject to change without prior notice.

Please enclose a cheque or postal order made payable to *Bookpoint Ltd*, and send to: Hodder Children's Books, 39 Milton Park, Abingdon, OXON OX14 4TD, UK. Email Address: orders@bookpoint.co.uk

If you would prefer to pay by credit card, our call centre team would be delighted to take your order by telephone. Our direct line *01235 400414* (lines open 9.00 am–6.00 pm Monday to Saturday, 24 hour message answering service). Alternatively you can send a fax on *01235 400454*.

TITLE		FIRST NAME		SURNAME	

ADDRESS	
DAYTIME TEL:	POST CODE

If you would prefer to pay by credit card, please complete:
Please debit my Visa/Access/Diner's Card/American Express (delete as applicable) card no:

Signature ....

Expiry Date: ....

If you would NOT like to receive further information on our products please tick the box. ❐